... And when Kate turned to Lauren, something about the way she was standing and the light in the office, which was coming only from the windows and the skylight (and there was a particularly spectacular Los Angeles evening sky), something about all of it plus Lauren's natural beauty combined to make the reality of Lauren eclipse the fantasy.

Kate wanted to tell Lauren she looked beautiful but no words came to her. There was more than physical beauty. The room changed for Kate when Lauren walked in. Kate opened her mouth, closed it again. No way to tell Lauren what she felt at that moment. And yet somehow she knew that there was no need to tell her. She wanted to go to Lauren and didn't know what was holding her back. Neither of them moved. They stood across the room from each other but they could have been touching.

FOR KEEPS

a novel by
Elisabeth Nonas

the NAIAD PRESS inc.
1985

Printed in the United States of America
First Edition

Cover design by Tee A. Corinne
Typesetting by Sandi Stancil

Library of Congress Cataloging in Publication Data

Nonas, Elisabeth C., 1949–
  For keeps.

  I. Title.
PS3564.045F6 1985   813'.54   85-15559
ISBN 0-930044-71-1

Elisabeth Nonas was born in New York City in 1949. She majored in English at Vassar; her thesis was a collection of her own poetry. After college, she intended to be a film-maker. Towards that end, she went to graduate film school. Three years later, armed with a degree and an award-winning eighteen-minute film, she left New York City for Los Angeles, where she writes for television.

She lives with her lover and is active in gay politics.

FOR KEEPS is her first novel.

for Carole
(who got it started and kept it going)

PART I

Eyes wide open after sex. Wide open in the dark. Nothing to see. Nothing she wanted to think about. Trying to make sense out of the shapes in this strange room. Not her room. Things played tricks on her in the dark, changed shape. At night, everything a frightening puzzle. The body that loomed near the bed watching them, in the morning would be recognized as her shirt draped over a chair.

Kate lay on her back, head propped awkwardly against the wall. She was comfortable enough. Next to her, Hilary shifted position. Her back to Kate, she pulled her legs up closer to her body, curling deeper into her dreams. After making love they had fallen asleep wrapped in each other, but turned away during the night, each used to sleeping alone.

Hilary's cat prowled around the bed. Kate sensed she was sleeping in the cat's place. It was a challenge of wills. The cat staring at Kate from the top of the dresser, ready to jump onto the bed; Kate glaring her message: Set one paw on this bed and you're a dead cat.

Kate put her hand on Hilary's shoulder, rubbed her back. A gesture of propriety for the cat's benefit. And not so much a loving gesture as a reality check. She didn't want to be wide awake. She wanted to be asleep and close and in love. But these days she made do with what she had: strange cats, strange rooms.

She must have slept a little. The cat was curled near her feet. Kate didn't remember falling asleep, wasn't aware of having stopped thinking. Hilary moaned, tossed her head. She was having a bad dream.

Kate turned to her, stroked her back, her hair, made soothing noises. Hilary didn't turn towards her, but she quieted down. Kate rested her hand, outside the covers, on Hilary's hip. (She would have gathered Anne to her, kissed her awake to make sure the nightmare was gone, then kissed her back to sleep. But that was Anne, who couldn't lose her dreams without waking.) Kate spooned around Hilary, not guardian of her sleep.

Kate tore three pages off her pad. She took a sip of coffee, uncapped her fountain pen, and held it over the page. This was supposed to get the words flowing. She had turned off the typewriter. Maybe if she didn't have its hum reminding her that she wasn't writing, something would come.

She was stuck on her movie for television about a woman on a wilderness survival trip for women over thirty. The network executive in charge of the production didn't think the first draft had enough action. "It just didn't play for me," was exactly how he had put it to Kate's agent. Kate had a feeling that he was the kind of man for whom no scene in what he called a "women's film" would play, but she had to do her best to put in more action.

She looked at the clock. Three hours before she had to be at the studio.

The scene she wanted was stretching away from her. It

was in front of her, in a long tunnel, or at the other side of one.

She had described the feeling to Anne once: like trying to get her fingers out of the woven straw tubes given as party favors when she was little. The harder she pulled, the more the straw would stretch and tighten around her fingers. The only way to extricate herself was to let go.

Knowing well all the tricks to get out of being blocked, she typed her name, the date, how it felt to be stuck. Then the problem she was having, describing the script as it was and the scene she couldn't bring to life. By the time she had finished playing with her thoughts, she had enough of a burgeoning idea to keep the network happy. She looked at the clock. Thirty-five minutes until her meeting — just enough time to shower, if she didn't dry her hair.

As she undressed, Kate thanked heaven she worked well under deadlines.

Neil's office was on the first floor and faced the parking lot. Throughout their meeting he kept swivelling in his chair to look longingly at his car, a Studebaker Commander in 50's aqua. He was no more receptive to the new scene than he had been to the original idea. "I mean, I like it," he said, with a glance out the window, "but it sounds like I've seen it before, know what I mean?"

When she got home and called her agent to report on the meeting, Nancy was sympathetic. "I was afraid he'd be like this. He won't be around much during shooting, though. I hope."

"He said something else I didn't like," Kate said.

"What?"

"That we're not going into production until they find a more bankable lead."

"Surely that isn't news to you."

"Well no, but I just thought, I guess I just hoped they'd see that the story is enough to hold it all together. Without a bankable star."

"They just want to do the script justice. Ignore Neil. Relax, enjoy the break. Think of it as a vacation."

"I don't want a vacation."

Kate didn't just "not want" a vacation, she dreaded one. If it had come a year ago, maybe she and Anne could have worked things out. It certainly wouldn't do her any good now.

From Nancy's office, Kate drove out to the beach. Even though she'd lived in L.A. for seven years, she still couldn't take the beaches for granted. Being a New Yorker, she had always thought that going to the beach was something one did only with much planning, and only on vacation. It meant getting out of the City. If you wanted the exotic beaches in Jamaica or the Bahamas, it often involved airplanes. The beach was definitely not something you got to in twenty minutes.

When she had first met Anne, Kate hated lying in the sun, although she liked the way she looked with a tan. But Anne liked to spend whole days at the beach, and Kate had learned to adjust.

Once, she read every magazine that had lain around the house for weeks, while Anne stretched out on the sand next to her and slept. At the end of the day Anne was a glorious bronze.

"See! What's the point?" Kate complained. "We were out there the same amount of time and look at you." They were lying on the bed, after their shower. Kate pointed to Anne's tan line, then put her finger on her one affected area, her nose, which was very red. "Compared to this."

Anne answered very calmly. "You were reading."

"The *sun* did not know I was reading!"

"You weren't concentrating. It makes a difference."

Kate smiled thinking back on it. She had since met several other people who held the same theory.

And she herself had changed. Not to the point of being able to spend hours lying on the beach; but the laid-back L.A. lifestyle all her New York friends had teased her about had finally gotten to her. She had dumped her car, a practical Honda, and bought her first convertible: a cream-colored Alfa Romeo Spider.

And she spent a lot of time at the beach. Not to get a tan, but to walk out the stories in her head, get a good fix on new plot ideas. Or to let off steam, work out the knots. She would walk or skate or grab a bite to eat at one of the many restaurants or fast food places lining Ocean Front Walk.

Venice was like other beaches in that sand stretched to surf. But there all similarities ended. Ocean Front Walk, a street closed to cars, meandered alongside the beach and was a haven for sun bathers, cyclists, skaters, strollers, gawkers. Kate liked the mix of people: senior citizens, artists, junkies, aging hippies, locals and tourists. Venice was not like any beach in New York (or even California). It was the Sixties' Last Stand.

Kate parked in a lot facing the ocean. She sat on the curb near her car as she laced up her skates. The air was clear; she could see up the coast past Santa Monica all the way to Malibu.

Closing her eyes, she took a deep breath; letting it out didn't make her feel any better. She kept telling herself this restlessness was about her script, that she had just busted her ass to meet her deadline, was eager to get going, and she was feeling a natural disappointment at the letdown.

She could have believed herself if every woman who passed didn't somehow remind her of Anne. One had the same light brown hair, another the same body type, lean and boyish. Another pushed her hair out of her eyes with the same gesture Anne used. Kate sat on a bench and looked out towards the water but couldn't help noticing women. She focused on a smile, a posture, a figure. A woman on a twelve-speed, wearing tight spandex cycling pants and a helmet — how serious she was, speeding along the bike path. Another on a funky fat-wheeled beach cruiser, riding barefoot, singing at the top of her lungs.

Kate studied them and others. Tried to guess what they did that enabled them to be at the beach in the middle of the day. Several women in bikinis skated by, each one displacing the last in Kate's mind.

Anne crossed in and out of her thoughts. That had been happening more often lately, to Kate's consternation. Their two-and-a-half year relationship had ended six months earlier. Long enough, Kate figured, for her to be well out of the heartbreak and into getting on with her life.

Her main strategy had been to keep busy. And it had worked pretty well. She would forget for a while, be reminded again, then feel better again. The initial pain had almost been worse than the pain she felt after her mother died — as if it were harder to miss someone when you knew she was still around. Every time she thought she was used to not seeing Anne they would run into each other, or Anne would call. Something would set Kate back again. She spent a great deal of time avoiding Anne, trying to second-guess whether or not she would be at a party or a bar. Wanting to avoid her and wanting to see her. Wanting now to be much later.

She got up and skated away from these thoughts. She was past all that now. She'd been feeling good lately, busy with work and friends. She sped along the concrete, past the shops and restaurants, and let the view of the water and the heat from the sun soothe her.

A woman skated by in the skimpiest of bikinis, gold lamé that glistened as she flew past. She jumped and pivoted, landed skating backwards, and continued as smoothly as if she were on ice. Kate smiled.

A good romance. Several of her friends were advocating that. Someone to take her mind off Anne. When they had heard she was available, they were only too eager to set her up: "I know this lawyer," or "You should meet —" or "Do you know —?" But she hadn't been ready for that and the few dates she had had were dismal failures.

She had gone out with her friends to the bars. Had watched women, danced with them. But none of them was Anne. And some of them had reminded her too much of Anne. The inevitable comparisons had resulted in keeping Kate far away from everything but her work. And even there she had noticed a distance that was unusual for her. Her pain was seeping into everything, even the lightest scene she wrote contained a slight sad undercurrent.

Kate stopped at an outdoor restaurant for an espresso.

On this beautiful day the restaurant was crowded. A lot of people were playing hooky from work. They looked dressed up in their work clothes, too many clothes for the beach, serious colors, but at least they were taking advantage of the day. Kate sat at a table sipping her espresso, blind to any advantages. She could have been sitting in the dark. Coming out here had had the opposite effect from what she had hoped.

She had an image of her life. It was like a book. Only what she was reading/doing was printed on tracing paper, and the real text, her thoughts and feelings, was on paper under that — her daily life superimposed on what was going on inside. Like here at the beach: she watched everyone walk by, saw a few women she thought were cute, or she sat at a café and ordered lunch, exchanging pleasantries with the waitress, deciding what to have — and underneath all that was the thought of Anne, a constant nagging to have her there, at least have her present in some sense other than in this continuous ache.

And yet she knew that time wouldn't have helped a year ago, either. By then they had needed more than time.

Kate took a deep breath and let it out, and felt a little better. There was more room out here than she thought. And she could see for herself — not just from the number of people who were at the beach — that it was, indeed, a beautiful day.

After she put her skates back in the car she still wasn't ready to leave, so she walked on the beach. She thought about what she'd been like since Anne moved out. Objectively, as if it had happened to someone else.

For the first time, she saw that the tracing paper effect had been a constant. Her daily activities were printed on the thinnest paper. The main text of the book that was her life was only about Anne. With good friends, Jennifer or Claire, she had been honest — "I can't stand it, I miss her so much." With casual friends she had mostly listened, turning pages about Anne while they talked about something else.

Even sleep had been a dangerous place. Her dreams had been little more than memories of Anne's presence, sometimes no more than Kate and Anne and a white wall.

It was still a puzzle to her that she had been able to get any work done. When she had tried to write, Anne was mixed in the ink of her pen and kept coming out on paper in characters who weren't anything like Anne but who suddenly had her eyes or her laugh or her hands.

Before she became a graphic artist, Anne had done a

lot of ceramic work and her hands were potter's hands, always molding and shaping, testing forms. Kate gave them to one of her characters and then took them back for herself, remembering those hands on her body. Never still. Moving, touching, not so much stroking as finding a place and pressing, gently but firmly, then moving to another. On her stomach, her inner thighs. Even as they were falling asleep one hand still tentatively moving over her body, with less frequency, less regularity.

She looked back with amazed detachment at those days and nights. Watched herself shower and dress and meet someone for lunch or go to the cleaners or fantasize about a woman in a sportscar who passed her on the freeway. As if life were going on.

Her house, where she wrote and spent most of her time, had become an enemy reminding her of Anne, of their life together. So she worked to remove all traces of Anne. She spread her own clothes into Anne's closet. Anne's study, which doubled as the guest room, was the hardest hit. Kate rearranged what furniture was left, and stayed out of that room. Her own office was the least affected: with the exception of the empty spaces where photographs of Anne had been displayed, nothing had changed.

Even the exterior of her house had looked different to her, somehow reflecting the new emptiness inside.

Because she hadn't been ready to be home alone, she had spent time with people she hardly knew. With a group of single women who ran out to the bars as if they were important places to be. All denying that they thought they would meet anyone interesting there (probably true), but none of them ever missed a Wednesday or a Saturday (those were the most popular nights). As caught up as they in the desperation, the need to be doing something every minute, she went with them partly in self-defense, determined to have a better time than Anne, wherever she was, was having.

Thank God for Jennifer, thought Kate, as she drove to see her.

Jennifer who was almost boring in her stability. And who had pulled Kate through her darkest hours.

Jennifer and Eve had a house and children and a life. Everything that Kate associated with being safe and warm and nothing that she had at the moment.

The happiest of any of Kate's friends, Jennifer and Eve had been together for eight years. She would joke with them about being old married ladies, set in their ways, no fun. But she envied them. No matter how much her single friends droned on about how they preferred being alone, Kate believed that most of them were after exactly what Eve and Jennifer had. None of them was alone and content; each was alone and cruising.

Part of cruising, of new beginnings, the thrill and excitement of that lifestyle, Kate thought, was really the thrill of possibility. That this could be it, maybe this would be the one. That's what they were all after, she believed. And what so many settled for was sex instead of true intimacy (not that intimacy precluded sex, or vice versa, just that often sex was confused with intimacy).

Eve was a therapist. Kate loved her because she was a total space cadet, with so many ideas going on in her head at once that it was often difficult to understand her. Only half of each idea seemed to come out of her mouth, the other half staying in her head. Kate always wondered how Eve's clients made sense of what she said. Very often, Kate had to ask questions to get the full effect of what Eve was talking about, like putting together a puzzle or filling in the blanks.

They lived in a big house on a quiet street in Santa Monica, about ten blocks from the beach. Jennifer's children, Diane who was ten and Allison who was twelve, adored Eve, and it was obvious they were adored in return. They were always bringing their friends home, so the house was usually full of kids and pets and bicycles.

Jennifer was politically active, and the children's books she wrote and illustrated translated her feminist philosophy into words and pictures without being preachy.

Jennifer's studio, a big airy room over the garage, was filled with paints and pencils and inks and brushes. And found objects: rocks, dried flowers, pieces of wood that intrigued Jennifer with their shapes and shadows. Photographs and postcards and the children's paintings were tacked onto every inch of wall.

To Kate, Jennifer's studio was heaven. Smells of oils and turpentine and fixitive. The studio seemed so much more alive than her own office, her own desk covered with papers and pads and pens. No other senses were present in the act of writing — not unless she conjured them up. No smell, no colors, just the scratching of her pen on the paper, the intrusive clatter of her typewriter.

Lately she had spent several mornings in Jennifer's studio, curled in a chair in the corner reading while Jennifer sketched.

When Kate arrived from the beach, Jennifer was in the back yard weeding the vegetable garden (a former project of Allison's, dropped into her mother's unwilling lap). As Jennifer worked, she urged Kate to go to a party given by a mutual friend.

"I hate parties, Jennifer."

"It'll be good for you."

"I won't know anyone."

"That's the *point* of it, dummy. Emily said she's expecting between thirty and forty women."

Jennifer lectured until Kate finally gave in and agreed to go to the party. She declared it her official re-entry to the world of the living.

* * * * *

To her surprise, Kate had enjoyed herself. Maybe because after the bars, where everything was noise and surface, shorthand (where Kate would keep herself from dancing with a woman by saying "I don't like her shoes"), here was a chance to talk to some women and not worry about creating a front.

At a bar, she'd fall into bar formula. She had to be clever, hot, she had to learn to strike a pose while pretending not to. She had to pretend also that she wanted to be there, or didn't care what happened while she was there.

No one pretended anything at Emily's old house in Silver Lake. About fifty women, some dressed in slacks and silk shirts, some in more trendy fashions, were talking to each other, in groups, in pairs. Real conversations. Kate stuck pretty close to people she knew at first.

She watched Emily scuttle from group to group, making sure everyone had drinks and food. Kate was jealous of Emily's ease in a crowd. Maybe it had something to do with the aggressiveness of her work, Kate reasoned. Emily was an executive recruiter, a headhunter, luring executives from one well-paying job to another, more lucrative job.

Emily wasn't a close friend, like Jennifer. More of a buddy. Kate had met Emily in a bar six years earlier. Emily had come up to a group of women Kate was with and introduced herself and Deborah, her lover at the time, saying they were new in town and didn't know too many people. A year or so after that, Deborah had left Emily for another woman. Broke Emily's heart.

Kate's thoughts were interrupted as Emily took her arm and, accusing her of not "mingling," dragged her into another room.

That was how Kate met Hilary.

Hilary was an attorney specializing in real estate law. For a long time, she and Kate exchanged standard party talk — what they did, who they knew, where they came from — but then they were talking and joking and Kate found herself attracted to this woman. The first since Anne. They danced and talked more and separated and got back together and separated again. Kate was aware of Hilary all through the party. She could feel her on the other side of the room, Hilary's blue blouse a flash of color out of the corner of her eye. Kate heard Hilary laughing in the kitchen and went in to get another drink.

In the center of a group of five or six women, with everyone's attention focused on her, Hilary was telling a story, elaborately acting it out. Kate was sure Hilary noticed that she was watching her; but like an actress who instinctively knows when the camera is on her and changes posture and facial expression to best advantage, Hilary gave no outward sign.

When she was ready to leave, Kate looked around for Hilary, wanting to get her phone number, at least say goodbye. But Hilary was nowhere to be found. Someone said she had left. A little surprised, Kate reflected that maybe because of her attraction to Hilary she had misinterpreted what had gone on between them.

The next day she played it back for herself: how close Hilary had stood when they talked, how she had put her hand on Kate's arm to make a point. Seductive touches, a very quick caress, a glance, a seemingly accidental brush of Hilary's lips on Kate's neck as she leaned over to whisper something. Hilary was the one to suggest they dance, had moved close to Kate (she wore a perfume that seemed like a memory, of that Kate was sure). Her look had said she was available.

It all added up. Still, nothing had happened, nothing had been said.

Just when Kate had convinced herself that she'd imagined all of it, Hilary called and they made a date. Very nonthreatening: dinner and a movie. So Kate hadn't been totally off-base; Hilary had been interested enough to call Emily for her number.

Hilary met Kate right after work. Kate liked the way she dressed. Kate would learn that even when Hilary wore what she called her basic dress-for-success suit there was a difference, a flair that marked the rest of her wardrobe as well. This first night Hilary wore a soft cotton shirt with a wing collar, tweed pants, a heavy wool shawl collar sweater. She looked great, but something about her said don't touch.

They had dinner at an Italian restaurant in West Hollywood before going to see a Katherine Hepburn film. Over espresso, Hilary told Kate that although she was attracted to her she was dating other women, and would not sleep with her. Because it confused things, she said. Because intelligent women started acting like thirteen-year-olds as soon as sex was involved.

But when the lights went down in the theatre Hilary leaned towards Kate and slid her hand over Kate's thigh and kept it there even after the lights came up again.

The rest of Kate's date with Hilary was talk on Hilary's part and lust on Kate's. Hilary had reasons and excuses for what she was and wasn't doing with her life. Kate didn't listen to a lot of it because she was very turned on. Or she listened to it but didn't really believe it because Hilary's actions didn't mesh with her words, beginning from the moment they had waited to buy tickets.

Hilary had unbuttoned the top of her blouse and loosened her collar. Kate was so surprised at the effect of that simple, spontaneous gesture, especially after the lecture on distance, that it caught her off guard. Maybe there was promise here, not just tease.

Hilary kissed Kate in the car. Kate realized this was the first woman she had kissed since Anne. For a few moments Kate wasn't sure who she was holding or what she was doing but then Anne in and Anne out as Hilary's lips opened and her tongue teased Kate's. Kate didn't know whether to do more or less and just when she decided she wanted more Hilary pulled away saying, "I've got an early meeting."

It didn't occur to Kate to weigh all she'd heard Hilary say against what Hilary actually did because the kiss was the loudest memory of that evening.

After that night, whenever they saw each other, Hilary teased and flirted and came on very strong — but they didn't go to bed together.

At lunch one day Hilary did her usual, then, on the way back to their cars, kissed Kate in the parking lot.

"What are you trying to do?" Kate demanded, pulling away.

"What's the matter?" Hilary asked coyly. "Are you shy?" She tried to get close to Kate again.

"No. But don't do that if you don't want more."

Of course that was easy for Kate to say. She knew Hilary was playing with her and the game suited Kate's purposes just fine for the moment. After their first date, their heavy kissing and exploring in the car, Hilary would see Kate only sandwiched between other appointments, when she had to get back to a client. Not that they didn't do lovely things like lunch or breakfast at the beach, an afternoon espresso, a stolen hour or so wherever. They would talk and flirt and Kate was very safe in pretending to both of them that she wanted more.

A few days later, Kate visited Jennifer. As they walked out to Jennifer's yard, Kate said, "It's nice to spend time with someone sane." They stretched out on lounge chairs crowded near newly planted rows of vegetables and sipped lemonade.

Kate closed her eyes and rested her head on the back of the chair. "God, this feels good. I never sit outside at my house anymore." Because breakfast and the papers in the yard on Sundays belonged to Anne and another life.

"Whatever happened with Susan?" asked Jennifer. She and Eve had introduced Kate to a colleague of Eve's.

"She kept trying to analyze why we weren't going to bed together."

"How's it going with Hilary?"

"Okay, I guess."

Actually, she had stayed away from Hilary since that episode in the parking lot. She knew this was a game, she admitted to Jennifer, she also knew she didn't care — so why not play? It cost her nothing, no emotions invested. And, should it happen that they slept together, it would light a little corner of a night. "Well, not light it so much as fill it," she confessed.

She concluded her discussion of Hilary with "She isn't sure if she wants to be involved."

"And you do?"

Kate had to laugh. "I hadn't really thought about it that way."

Jennifer invited her to stay for dinner. Kate rarely refused becuase she loved spending time with the kids, but tonight she wanted only to go home and collapse. "A good soak in a hot tub. I've been looking forward to it all day." She could do that now that she wasn't always so frantic to be busy every minute. Now that the initial desperate stage had passed.

It would have been a wonderful evening if the phone hadn't rung. Or if she hadn't answered it. A newly developed second sense told her before she picked up the receiver that Anne would be at the other end of the line.

Kate kept her voice firm. "I asked you not to call." Not that she was surprised that Anne had called with something "important." At first it had been any excuse — did you find my gray shorts? Did anything come from my bank? It had been over a month since they had seen each other, but only two weeks since Kate had said don't call.

"It's important."

"It's always important." Kate had no patience for this.

"This time it really is."

Kate was angry at Anne for calling and at herself for not being angry enough and hanging up immediately. "Well?"

"I got a promotion," Anne said.

Kate was so attracted to the hint of intimacy in Anne's voice that she didn't define the apologetic tone until later, and therefore missed its warning. As it was, everything disappeared for a moment. Only for a moment. There was so much riding on this that maybe it meant nothing at all. Did she really care?

They'd been through so much about Anne's promotion, with Anne working extra hours and Kate helping by taking care of little things and staying out of her way so Anne could concentrate. They had planned a big celebration when the promotion finally came through — a weekend in San Francisco, dinner at Chez Panisse. This was *her* celebration too. Kate couldn't absorb what she was hearing, her mind was racing. Thoughts popped into her head — she's calling to make arrangements. After all, you helped me so much, she'd say. Then Kate would censor herself only to have another thought pry itself out from under her grip. She wasn't expecting another shoe to drop. Then it fell.

"They're moving me to New York."

The sensation was like falling out of the tree at her grandfather's house when she was six. She'd landed belly across a lower branch, the wind knocked out of her.

Kate heard everything else as if Anne spoke in a foreign

language. She couldn't translate all the words, but some main points floated to her through the fog. Anne was to design a corporate identity for a new computer software firm. Design director for the project. They were grooming her for creative director, she was sure of it. Everything she'd wanted. Then vaguely familiar words came over the wire; Anne was talking about something else.

What Kate was hearing was a bad memory and she couldn't figure out why Anne kept talking about it. Gifford Kates and Dunn. One of the biggest New York ad agencies. What did this have to do with Anne's no longer being in L.A.? Kate remembered just as Anne said it.

"She was the account exec from Gifford Kates and Dunn who was out here last spring."

And then English spoken again as Kate realized that Anne was telling her that she was involved with this woman. Jane. Jane and Anne were lovers. Plain English. A cold hard language, word after word that Kate couldn't help but understand, couldn't block if she tried.

Kate was in the car before she realized she'd hung up on Anne. She had said something before slamming down the receiver and throwing the phone across the room, but didn't remember what. She knew only that she had to leave. But she couldn't go anywhere. She just sat in her car in her garage.

Jane had been a figure in the background when Kate and Anne had started fighting. Jane and Anne had had drinks one night. Maybe something else, too. Kate would never know. Hadn't she suspected something at the time, pushed it out of her head? Maybe she hadn't thought anything at all. Maybe none of this really mattered to her now. She'd call Hilary, see her.

They must think she was a jerk, a fool. Anne had betrayed her. She wanted to kill both of them. She thought of the time she had spent thinking about being back with Anne, and couldn't believe how naive she had been. She wanted to hurt Anne as much as she herself hurt. Instead she pummelled the steering wheel and the seat next to her until her hand was red and throbbing.

That brought the tears and rage. And memory. She remembered what she'd said to Anne. "Who else did you have to fuck for the job?"

That had been Tuesday.

Saturday, the night before Anne was going to leave for New York, the night Kate ended up with her eyes wide open in the dark, she slept with Hilary for the first time.

Hilary tried to talk Kate into keeping the relationship as it was, even though they were attracted to each other, but Kate wouldn't listen to any of it. She drove straight through until she got what she wanted which was what she was pretty sure that Hilary, under all her double talk, wanted also.

Making love with someone who wasn't Anne wasn't as hard as Kate had thought it would be. She was amazed at how different Hilary felt from Anne.

It had been months since the break up, so long that Kate didn't realize that she had forgotten what Anne felt like until she felt someone who wasn't Anne.

There were the inevitable comparisons. But not unfavorable. Anne would have touched her this way, but oh, this was nice. The softness of this new woman, entering her and exploring, held Kate. She had found another hiding place, a sanctuary.

If she thought of Anne she buried deeper into Hilary. Deeper at the thought of Jane, also. Hilary was beautiful and sexy. She straddled Kate's hips, closing her eyes as she moved. Then she leaned over Kate and Anne was not there at all.

Afterwards, Kate lay in the dark, eyes wide open.

Anne would be up packing. She always waited until the

last minute. Sometimes Kate had packed for her.

Anne was like her child in some ways. Maybe that was the trouble with having children. They grew up and left.

Kate jolted herself back to the present with a thought of Anne and Jane together. Of Anne packing to go to Jane.

She stroked Hilary's back, kissed her neck until she woke up. She had caught Hilary off guard, too stuck in sleep to remember to hold herself back. They made love again. Kate pressed into Hilary to wipe everything else out of her mind. It almost worked.

"You're very quiet tonight." Claire said the words as a question that Kate could answer or not.

Claire's subtle concern was the quality Kate most appreciated in her friend. They had only known each other two years, but rarely had Kate met anyone with whom she was so immediately comfortable. People introduced to them thought they'd been friends forever. Some even wondered why they had never become lovers.

Claire was a film editor. Kate thought that organizing footage helped Claire to stay focused on the big picture, make sense out of seemingly disparate events. Claire more than anyone except Jennifer had helped Kate when Anne moved out. The day Anne came back to the house to pick up her things, Claire took Kate out to lunch. Kate could — and often did — call her at any hour. Claire was patient and caring, listening to her obsess about Anne until even Kate had grown bored.

They sat at a sushi bar in Westwood. Three chefs worked behind the counter performing astounding feats with their long knives, the one closest to them transforming a cucumber into an arrangement of wafer-thin slices in the shape of a rose.

"They're like human Cuisinarts," Kate observed. Then,

realizing she hadn't responded to Claire's non-question, "I'm sorry. I'm distracted."

"Don't apologize."

"I'm going crazy. Pretty soon I'll need a hat to keep them voices in." This was a reference to Claire's theory on why crazy people wear hats.

"What about Hilary?"

"What about Hilary?"

"Doesn't she help at all?"

Kate was hard pressed to describe *what* that relationship did for her. If in fact she could even call it a relationship. It verged on hot and heavy when they were together. Sometimes. After their first night together there had been others. They talked on the phone a lot, made love, went out for dinner.

But as they spent more time together Hilary's coyness did not dissipate. She was a master at it. She was warm and flirtatious, promising and delivering just enough to keep Kate coming back for more.

They would go out and have — at least Kate had thought at the time that they had — a nice evening. They would talk the next day about doing something else, and Hilary would say she wasn't sure when they could get together, how about lunch soon.

"I was hoping for dinner." Kate was really hoping to make love to her again.

"I can't this week. How about Monday?"

"Okay," Kate would say.

Then Hilary would change Monday to Tuesday. Or call Kate on Monday at the last minute and they'd get together. Kate didn't know why she kept calling. Maybe because it was easier than trying to meet someone else.

And, on the surface, Hilary was very attractive. And every so often she would do something that would hook Kate. Something like the gesture she had made on their first date, when she had loosened her collar. Something so spontaneous that Kate would think, there's a chance to get to know this person. But for the most part, the only reminder of Hilary was a slight waft of her perfume on Kate's clothes.

"Where'd you go?" Claire waved her hand across Kate's line of sight.

"I'm sorry."

"Quit apologizing! I just want to make sure you're okay."

"I'm fine. Just antsy. Let's go." Kate paid for dinner and they left.

Westwood Village, clustered below the UCLA campus, was crowded with students on their way to dinner or the movies or on ice cream or cookie runs. The town's shops and restaurants and movie theatres made the area very convenient and walkable, but Kate's main complaint about Westwood was that it was too clean-cut, too collegiate. However, she kept looking at women and pointing them out to Claire.

"They're not my type," said Claire. "Too cute and too young. What would you talk about?"

"Who wants to talk?"

A pretty, young UCLA student walked by. Kate watched her, turned to look after she passed them. Claire took her arm, dragged her toward the parking lot. "Too young and too straight."

Kate glanced back one last time. "But that's my specialty."

"That's your problem."

But that was only the manifestation of the problem. Whatever the real problem was, it had been with Kate since the break-up. Then, she'd been too busy to pay much attention. She had only noticed out the corner of her eye that she was at a great distance from her scripts, wasn't totally involved in them.

It was even worse now, with her project on hold. She had taken herself to the beach, to stores, anything to get away. No matter what she did or where she went, when she came home she was disappointed. Something should have happened. She was missing something. Without work as a focus, all she was aware of was women. She fell in love with their perfume, a haircut, a shirt. Everywhere she went, the same.

That night, after the movie with Claire, Kate ran a bath, then settled herself into the very hot water determined to sort it all out.

She and Claire were in almost the same position, both on the tail end of break-ups, and had talked a lot about their relative situations during dinner. They had also noticed women, each and every one, it seemed, and delivered editorials on them all. Just something to pass the time, take their minds off themselves.

Alone, Kate thought it was more than that.

Something kept running in her head. Not an idea, but the form of an idea. Not a person, but the form of a person. True Love. A perverse sort of Muse that didn't inspire Kate to work, but rather did its best to distract her, take her mind off what she'd been doing, or what she was supposed to be doing. Then it set her down in a jungle of women.

True Love created an itching in the center of her palms. A need to be filled up. She wanted to cup a lover's nipples, caress her hip, thigh, the nape of her neck. True Love did this to her even when there was no one else around, underlining the absences in Kate's life.

Kate ran more water into the tub.

She had begun to recognize True Love everywhere she looked. In restaurants, in stores, even in her living room.

Eve and Jennifer had come over for a drink before they

all went out to dinner, and though the couple didn't sit next to each other in Kate's living room, Kate felt True Love bouncing off her walls, knocking into the furniture, slipping its warm hands under her clothes and rubbing against her legs. "Let me in, come on, it'll feel so good." It was very seductive.

Kate realized that that's what had made her long for Hilary, and for the women in Westwood, women she hadn't even met. Imaginary women, ones she had never seen. She longed for them more than for Hilary.

She saw True Love on TV, stopped watching. Saw it at the bars, stopped going. Heard it in songs, wouldn't listen. But she couldn't get away from it.

In the restaurant, Eve and Jennifer had sat across the table from Kate, who was crowded into her corner of the booth by True Love. No space between the lovers, Eve's arm around Jennifer's shoulders, Jennifer's hand some-where in Eve's lap. Kate felt like the fifth wheel even though her friends hadn't treated her like one. That was True Love's fault. It pointed things out to Kate: how vulnerable her back was without a hand caressing it, how empty the space was next to her.

Now that Kate had identified True Love, her life was dif-ferent. Instead of popping in and out, True Love was always there. It nudged her arm at the movies and asked, "You sure you like being here by yourself?"

"I do," said Kate. "Go away."

"Come on, wouldn't you rather have someone to lean against, whisper to?"

"I'm very happy, thank you."

Kate was never alone. True Love was always right over her shoulder. It was there from the first second after she opened her eyes in the morning, that blank moment when she had to place herself in the world. (And, not working, she needed to ask, what day is it? Why do I feel so lousy?

What did I do yesterday?)

By this time True Love was priming her for what might happen. "Maybe today. Maybe at the bank. Or the market. Or in a bookstore. Someone will be there. You may not notice her at first. But she will be there for you. It may be the most casual connection. Maybe even mistaking each other for friends of friends, you'll talk. . . ." Kate did her best to ignore True Love. She had an easier time if she kept busy.

One day she had a lunch date with Hilary and time to kill so she stopped in at Tower Records on Sunset Boulevard.

A dark-haired young woman at the information area was ripping open a new carton of records. A dyke. ("You think everyone's gay," Anne would accuse her. "No, just the ones who are," Kate would defend herself, "you can just tell.") She was joking with the guy at the information counter. He made her laugh and Kate found herself noticing the woman because of her laugh, the hoarse catch in her voice. She was wearing very tight jeans, sneakers, and a plain red sweatshirt with the sleeves cut off. The muscles in her arms were well defined. She must go to a gym, Kate thought.

[Immediately True Love is at her ear: "Beautiful, eh? Great body."]

Kate surprised herself by wondering what it would be like to be in bed with this athletic woman and hear her laugh.

[True Love: "Go ahead. Talk to her."]

But Kate wouldn't make any moves in that direction. In any direction, in fact, so the woman asked "Is there anything special you're looking for?"

Kate looked into brown eyes and an open, innocent face. "No. Thanks."

The woman went back to her conversation.

["Hot. Very hot. Look at her body."]

Kate moved to the reggae section.

The woman was just down the aisle, unpacking the

records. Kate noticed the curve of her bluejeaned ass as she squatted down to open a carton.

Quit it, Kate thought. But she didn't know if she was talking to herself or True Love. Kate managed to turn her gaze back to the records. She picked out a Bob Marley album and looked around. If she worked her way towards the Jazz section, she'd be away from that woman. Who certainly was cute.

Kate imagined them in the yard on a Sunday, lying in the sun, turning to each other, kissing lazily before beginning to make love.

"That's a good one."

Kate jumped.

"Sorry, I didn't mean to sneak up on you." The woman was standing next to Kate, who floundered for words. But she didn't have to say anything because after a glance at the album in Kate's hand, the woman flipped through the bin to another record: "This one's better," she said, and gave it to Kate. Then she left to help another customer.

Kate squeezed the record in her hand, smiled to herself. "I think I'm in love."

[True Love had been browsing around FEMALE VOCALISTS but was back to Kate in a flash. It ran its fingers along the back of her neck, her lower back, made her want other hands there, talking to her, caressing. True Love whispered in her ear: "Go get her. This is what you've been waiting for." Kate didn't budge. True Love wouldn't give up, either. "A drink. One little kiss. Wouldn't you like to touch her hand? Come on, I dare you." True Love nibbled at Kate's neck. "You used to be a charmer."

"Cut it out. I'm not interested."]

Kate took the record to the register.

"Let me know how you like it," the woman said as she rang it up. Her fingers grazed Kate's palm as she handed Kate her change.

"Thank you." Kate took her package and left.

She smiled all the way to the restaurant where she met Hilary. She was still smiling when she sat down.

"You look like the cat who ate the canary. What happened?" Hilary asked.

"Nothing. Just in a good mood, I guess. Want to go to your house and make love?"

"You *are* in a good mood."

"That's not an answer."

"I've got a client coming in at four."

"That's a no."

"Yes."

"So we'll eat something else. Waiter!"

The good mood lasted most of the afternoon. Hilary went back to her office and Kate went home.

She listened to the Bob Marley album and imagined what it would be like to dance with that woman from Tower Records.

"We've got to get you out of the house. Have some fun."

That's what Claire and Emily said when they showed up, unannounced, at Kate's early one evening.

"We are going to have a good time," Claire said.

"We are not going to sit around waiting for Hilary to call," Emily added.

They made Kate shower. When she protested that she had already done that, Claire explained, "This is a psychological shower."

"Do you a world of good," Emily said as she turned on the shower spray.

They waited for her in the living room. After Kate was dressed (and her friends had a say in that, too, picking out her sexiest black pants and a grey shirt they wouldn't let her button up all the way), they took her out to dinner.

By the time they got to West Hollywood, it was eleven-thirty and the bar was packed. Outside, Emily ran into some-one she knew, and stopped to talk to her. Claire and Kate (with True Love not far behind) went inside to get drinks and look around.

Kate sipped her beer and stood near the dance floor. She kept seeing things she didn't want to see. Private moments that were supposed to be lost in the crowd: a gesture or a kiss; a hand sliding inside a shirt; the beginning of a fight. She didn't want to be a part of these intimacies. She wanted to be absorbed in her imaginary woman, the one True Love was always teasing her with.

She saw Emily come inside. Kate watched her.

She was still amazed at Emily's ability to throw herself into a new group of women, take a flying leap and hit the ground talking.

Emily dated a lot. She was not aiming for any kind of permanence. No one stuck to her. She had her work and her friends and her women, always new. She was fast-talking with a corny sense of humor. She knew a million women and was always ready to introduce herself to another one. Women were always coming up to her and asking her to take them home. It always happened, and Kate couldn't get over it.

Like this night. Emily seemed to know everyone in the place. She worked the crowd like a professional, joking her way down to the end of the bar where Kate and Claire were standing.

"Claire," Emily scolded, "you're not supposed to let her do that." She had caught Kate staring into space.

"Come on," encouraged Claire, "we're here for a reason." She looked around the noisy, smoky room, scanning the women. Stationary cruising, Emily called it. "Look, that tall one."

"I already spotted her," Kate said unenthusiastically. "She's with the one in the black jacket."

"Okay." Claire looked around again, glimpsed a blonde in tight jeans and a cowboy shirt. "She's with that big group."

"I know the woman next to her," said Emily. "Want me to introduce you?"

"No." Kate didn't know either of them, but had seen them at bars, fundraisers, various gay political events. She had also seen them on one of the lots, either Paramount or CBS.

"Is she with that baby?" Claire couldn't believe it, kept staring. "How old is she, anyway?"

Kate didn't care. Inside all the noise, she heard her own voice: What am I doing here? She wasn't interested in these women. She could joke with Claire and Emily about which one she wouldn't kick out of bed, which one was to die for, but she wouldn't ever approach any of them. It was True Love that kept her there, standing behind her, grinding its pelvis into her in time to the music, putting its hands in her pants, teasing her. It cupped her ass, whispered to her about women on the dance floor.

Claire saw some women she'd met at a party a few weekends earlier, waved them over and introduced them to Kate and Emily. One of them, Diane, took an immediate interest in Kate, saying, "You must be from New York."

"How'd you know? I haven't opened my mouth."

"You have dark hair." When Kate didn't respond, Diane continued, pleased with her theory. "New Yorkers have dark hair, Californians have light hair."

"Then you must be from California," said Kate, pointing to Diane's light brown hair.

"Right!" she beamed, pleased that Kate had proved such a quick learner.

Kate was just about to whisper "Get me out of here" to

Claire when she heard hoarse laughter from the bar. She looked over and saw the woman from Tower. She wasn't alone, but Kate couldn't tell how "with" she and the other one were.

[True Love didn't miss a beat: "Go talk to her."]

Claire noticed that Kate was distracted. "See someone you know?"

"No. Well, not really. Do you know the one in the white jumpsuit?" Kate pointed out the woman to Claire.

"No. But she's cute. Who is she?"

"I don't know."

Later, having tactfully escaped Diane and her friend, Kate and Claire and Emily went back to the bar. Kate stood next to Claire's stool, and Emily sat on Claire's other side. When the woman from Tower walked by with her friend, a tall blonde in her early thirties, she saw Kate, waved hello and said, "Enjoy the Marley?"

The woman and her friend kept walking. Kate turned back to the bar and her beer. Emily and Claire waited for her to say something. She said nothing.

Claire was the more impatient of the two. "I thought you didn't know her."

"I don't."

"Then what was that all about?"

"Bob Marley."

"Very cute," said Claire.

"Who is she?" Emily asked Claire.

"She works at Tower Records," Kate said.

"What's her name?" Claire asked.

"Where does she work?" Emily couldn't hear very well from where she was sitting.

"Tower Records," explained Claire. But she hadn't finished with Kate. "So?"

"So?" Kate echoed.

"So who is she?"

"So I don't know."

"Are you going to find out?"

"Find out what?" Emily was getting more and more frustrated. "What's going on? Who *was* that woman?"

But Kate didn't want to talk. She suddenly felt like dancing and went and did so, with the blonde in the tight jeans and cowboy shirt whom Claire had pointed out earlier. Claire dropped the matter until right before they were going to leave, when she asked Kate, "Are you going to go out with her?"

"Right," Kate answered sarcastically.

Kate went outside to give the ticket for their car to the attendant. She had tried, unsuccessfully, to give True Love the slip. It stood next to her, the music still close around their heads even though they were outside.

The night was chilly. Kate's jacket was in Claire's car, but she stood still, thankful to be out of the smoke. She started to shiver and True Love put its arm around her. She shrugged it off. True Love stood a few feet away from her, miffed. Kate didn't have to worry about it because Claire and Emily joined her.

While they waited for Claire's BMW, Emily entertained the group of women who were also waiting, telling jokes and acting them out. She was applauded and cheered as she got into the back seat. One woman even leaned over as the car pulled away from the curb, throwing in her business card because Emily didn't have anything on which to write down her number.

"What does she do?" Kate asked.

Emily studied the card. "She's a loan officer at the Bank of America."

"That could come in handy."

"I suppose so," Emily said, looking back as her latest admirer rejoined the crowd.

True Love saved its lecture for Kate's ride home.

"You know, the one in the cowboy shirt couldn't take her eyes off you. And that tall one you were cruising would have come over sooner or later."

"I wasn't cruising anyone."

For once Kate was tired enough to be able to ignore True Love. She was also tired enough to think that although she had had fun tonight, she wanted her real place back. She wanted to curl up beside Anne and have her take away some of the night.

When she got home, she turned on the lights in every room. It was late, but she didn't think she could sleep. She thought of putting on the Marley album, but instead chose a new mystery novel. She took the book back with her through the house, turning off the lights.

The last thing she saw before she fell asleep was not the printed page, but that woman's dark eyes and long lashes.

Kate had lunch with Emily the next day.

"So. You enjoying your vacation?"

Kate just shrugged.

"Planning to go away at all?"

"I don't know. I've been working around the house." Cleaning out her office, which she no longer recognized now that she could see the top of her desk.

"What the hell kind of vacation is that? Get out of town for a while. That's what you need."

Kate figured there must be some truth to Emily's theory because everyone else thought the same thing. She'd been bombarded with offers: keys to a condo in Palm Springs, a cabin at Big Bear, a house on Lake Arrowhead.

Emily continued, "You won't be going back to work for a while. Why stick around and drive yourself crazy?"

"It's nice to just hang out at home for a change. No deadlines, nothing.

"Bullshit."

"And I don't want to go to the mountains, and I get bored in Palm Springs."

"So go to New York."

"Great. Maybe I could stay with Anne and Jane."

"You don't have to see them. Besides, you're going to have to get over that sooner or later. It's been —"

"Long enough and I know you're right and I don't want to go to New York."

"Have you spoken to her since she got there?"

"Are you my therapist?"

"Maybe if I were, you'd be feeling better by now."

"I feel fine. I just don't feel like running into her and her girlfriend."

"You're taking all this much too seriously. I'll bet that woman from last night could take your mind off things."

"Your loan officer?"

"No. That very cute one you talked to."

"I don't even know her name."

"Then go to the store and introduce yourself."

"You're good at that kind of thing, I'm not."

"It just takes a little practice. Come dancing with me Saturday, I'll give you cruising lessons."

The last thing in the world I want, thought Kate.

Emily launched into a pep talk. Kate knew the basic contents: go out, have a good time. Emily liked being single. Ever since Deborah left her. She'd gotten burned once and that was all she was going to allow. She chafed in a relationship. She had started going out again almost immediately, writing names and numbers of the women she'd met on the paper cocktail napkins from the bars. Five years later she was still collecting napkins. And still unattached. None of the women she dated had made it into the group of Emily's close friends to stay. Women came and went. Kate couldn't keep up with the procession.

[True Love couldn't resist a challenge. It glided over to Kate. "You could have your own procession." It put its hands on her shoulders. "You're a little tense, aren't you?" It started to massage her back. Kate tensed more. True Love whispered in her ear. "Relax. Take it easy." It ran its hands up and down her back, working around the vertebrae, kneading around the shoulder blades. Touched her everywhere with its sure hands.

It fingered her hair. Visions of a tall woman appeared in Kate's mind. True Love kissed her neck. More women appeared.]

Kate forced herself to get back to the conversation. Emily, having just reported the break-up of a couple they both knew, sighed, satisfied with the safety of her position, finished with relationships. She ended the conversation with the verbal equivalent of a wink and a nudge in the ribs: "Well, we don't have those problems and aren't we glad."

Emily's pep talk wasn't completely lost on Kate. She took her book and a folding chair and headed for the beach. She would try to relax, enjoy herself, not take everything so seriously. As she drove, images of Anne began to color the edge of her sight. She knew this was only another weak moment, not to be trusted or given serious attention. She thought of calling Hilary, finding out whether or not she could join her for the afternoon. Maybe a few hours in bed. But Kate didn't want to hear any excuses. A simple no would have been fine, but she knew Hilary would want to explain. The initial challenge had been interesting, but Hilary was getting to be a pain in the ass.

[True Love, in the back seat, threw up its hands in disgust. "When are you going to start listening to me?" And then it painted Kate such a vivid picture of the Tower Records woman that Kate was forced to pay attention. It was hard to stay sad when she was experiencing a slight shiver at a fantasy of waiting for that woman to come home to her after work, of making love in the shower.]

Kate let True Love take over from there. When they pulled into the Tower parking lot there was a spot right in front.

["Meant to be," True Love gloated.]

Kate lost her peripheral vision when she saw the woman behind the information counter. Nothing existed save that woman with her bright dark eyes, her athlete's body.

Introducing herself wasn't as hard as she had thought it would be. After all, there was now an unspoken bond between them. They each "knew." Their chance encounter at the bar the night before gave Kate information that otherwise might have taken her weeks to ascertain.

The woman's name was Nicky. She was twenty-six. (Kate could hear Claire teasing her about younger women. Emily would say "Nine years — so what's the big deal?")

Nicky was from L.A. She had lived with a woman for the past year.

"The one you were with last night?" (This was kind of like the "And is there a Mrs. Whoever?" straight women asked in the movies.)

Nicky laughed. "No. She's just a friend. Sandy was my lover and she moved to San Francisco."

"You didn't go?"

"She wanted me to. We broke up."

[True Love wasn't about to waste any more time. It stood right behind Kate, barely touching her, just enough so she could sense it there, its hands near her shoulders, moving downwards to outline the curves of her body. "Ask her out." Kate stepped sideways to get away from True Love. "Ask her out." A little louder this time.]

"Would you like to have dinner with me one night next week?" Kate occasionally surprised herself.

"Any night but Wednesday."

Oh my God, she's saying yes. Kate was alarmed and suddenly shy and embarrassed. "Tuesday?"

"Great. See you then."

She couldn't believe what she'd done. She took a walk on the beach just to let it sink in. She couldn't remember exactly what they had talked about because all she was left with was an image of Nicky in her jeans, faded dark green T-shirt, sneakers. Even Claire would have to say she was adorable.

Kate tried on five different shirts before she settled on the blue one she would wear to dinner with Nicky. She played the Marley album as she got dressed. She took a long time to do everything and still was ready with half an hour to spare. She called Jennifer and talked to her for a while but did not tell her about her date. (In case it didn't work out?)

Nicky's apartment was on Sweetzer off Santa Monica in West Hollywood. Kate parked half a block away, then sat in the car taking deep breaths and letting them out very slowly. She hated dating. What was the point? So much pretending.

[True Love told her she'd be late, opened the door for her. It waited in the car until Kate was in front of the building before following at a discreet distance.]

Kate guessed which door was Nicky's by the music coming from within the apartment. Loud and danceable. She didn't recognize the group. She rang twice before hearing footsteps. Then the music was lowered and the door opened.

Nicky stood partly concealed by the door. She was wrapped in a towel. She apologized for not being ready.

Kate looked everywhere but at Nicky's bare shoulders and legs.

"I'll only be a minute. Make yourself at home."

She kept talking from the bedroom as Kate studied the apartment. "Not much furniture, I know," Nicky said. "It went with Sandy to San Francisco. But all I really care about is the music."

That was obvious. The room was bare except for a couch and a director's chair with sagging canvas, but the stereo was state-of-the-art, its speakers big enough to fill a room five times the size of this one with music. There were no books around, only a pile of magazines, *Billboard,* a few old issues of *Rolling Stone.* Nicky's tape and record collection was the musical equivalent of Kate's bookshelves. A variety of tastes and categories.

"If you want something to drink, I think there's beer in the icebox. There may be some wine, too, but I doubt it."

"I'm fine, thanks," Kate called back. She sat on the floor to study the records. "This is quite a collection," she added but by then Nicky was in the room, and Kate didn't have to raise her voice. "Oh."

"I seem to keep sneaking up on you."

"You look great," Kate said. Kicked herself for sounding so trite. Even if it was true.

"Thanks."

Kate couldn't keep her eyes off Nicky. Even in loose-fitting pants and a white pullover she looked sexy.

Back to the records. That seemed safe. "You could open your own store."

"I love music. There are so many good records. There isn't enough time to listen to them all."

"I feel that way about books."

The restaurant was a fifteen-minute walk from the apartment. Kate was delighted at how easy it was to be with Nicky. A sweet fragrance hinted into the air. Nicky recognized and labeled it jasmine or mock orange. Kate confessed that although she'd lived in L.A. for seven years, she knew nothing about plants and trees.

Nicky asked Kate to tell her about growing up in New York, what it was like. She wanted to live there someday, though she liked L.A. because so much of the music industry was here. "But there are some great recording studios there," she went on, so as not to offend the native New Yorker. She went into an elaborate explanation of how the New York sound used to differ much more from the L.A. sound. "More urban, cosmopolitan. Though it was more of an energy than a physical sound. Tighter, more aggressive, you know. L.A. was a little more pop, easier." She concluded with, "Punk changed all that. Everything's more homogenized now. You can't always tell anymore. Know what I mean?"

Kate didn't, but it didn't matter. Nothing about the evening was complicated. They laughed a lot. Nicky told Kate about people who came into the store, celebrities, musicians, crazy people. Kate watched Nicky as she talked, kept thinking about her in that towel, and without the towel. Trying to listen to what Nicky was saying, she was more involved with the way she used her hands. Capable hands, long fingers. Kate thought maybe she should say something, not just sit there getting by with the vaguest of nods and agreements. But she was very happy to let Nicky talk, just to watch this new woman across the table from her. A new perfume, new colors, new associations.

Somewhere around the middle of the meal Kate knew that they would make love that night. Maybe it was when she took Nicky's hand — only for a second — that she had known for sure.

She had reached for Nicky without thinking. Probably because something Nicky had said made Kate want to touch her, be closer.

Maybe it was too soon. Both women blushed, made brief

eye contact, looked away. But once that had happened, there was no going back. Kate had butterflies in her stomach.

Midway through the main course they were ready to ask for the check. But they stayed and finished their meal. Rather, they sat until they couldn't stand it any longer and asked the waiter to take away their plates.

Kate put her hand on Nicky's back as they walked out.

[True Love watched them leave.]

They went back to Nicky's. For a long time they sat near each other on the couch and talked. Neither was uncomfortable, nor in a hurry. They didn't flirt. There was none of the back and forth that Kate had gotten from Hilary. As they talked they moved a little closer together. Nicky had put a Bill Evans tape into the machine. His music had never sounded so good.

Kate's hand was on Nicky's knee. They were facing each other. Nicky was wearing corduroy pants and Kate was running her fingers along the wales. If she ran her hand down Nicky's leg, the material looked lighter than it did when she ran her hand up the other way. She kept smoothing and roughing up the fabric. A constant rhythm that didn't end with the conversation and continued right into the kiss.

Kate leaned into it, her hand still on Nicky's leg. Her other hand went to Nicky's face, touched her hair. She pushed against Nicky, wanting her to lay back.

"No. Let's go to bed." Nicky stood up, took Kate's hand, and, turning off the light as they went, led her into the bedroom.

Kate was lost in Nicky. She knew only colors and the deepest softness. Nicky's body was alternately a shield and a well to fall into.

[True Love watched from the foot of the bed.]

Go away. Kate closed her eyes and True Love was gone

and Kate herself was gone, connected only to the woman lying with her. They were the same color as the night.

Kate slid her fingers into Nicky, who closed her eyes and tilted her pelvis so Kate was deeper inside. She murmured something that was lost to Kate.

[True Love reappeared.]

Kate pushed harder. Nicky moved faster under her hand, then guided Kate's head between her legs, holding her tightly as she pulled her closer.

Kate was aware only of her mouth on Nicky, her fingers inside her. Nicky grabbed Kate's shoulders, her head. Kate needed to be still deeper. She took hold of Nicky's hips to draw her closer, as if she could pull herself into Nicky.

Nicky was still, suspended. For a moment, only Kate continued to move. Then Nicky was shaking and crying, pulling Kate inside her. And just as suddenly pushing her away. Too much now. She collapsed, panting, one hand at her side, the other on Kate's head.

Kate kissed her way up Nicky's body, then she gently pulled away from Nicky and lay next to her.

Nicky, her head on Kate's shoulder, reached for her. Kate kissed the top of her head, stopped her hand. "Wait."

They lay quietly together.

Then Nicky slowly began to kiss Kate's neck. Kate tilted her head, allowing her easier access. But already Nicky was at her shoulder, her hip, back to her neck.

[Just before she came she felt a hand let go of her neck, release all the muscles in her back. Her body loosened. She barely heard the door close. Nicky's hand and mouth had driven True Love from the room. From Kate's life. The last thing it had said to her was "See, that's what I'd been talking about all along." But Kate wouldn't remember that until much later.]

* * * * *

When she got home the next morning there were no messages on her machine. Everything was as she had left it: yesterday's paper on the kitchen table, her coffee mug and breakfast dishes in the sink. No reminders of anyone else. She wouldn't have been able to tell she'd been gone if it weren't for the surreal quality morning takes on after a long night with a new lover.

They hadn't gotten more than three hours sleep, if that much.

Nicky had told Kate about Sandy. "She has a lot of energy and a lot of talent. She likes to start businesses, get them going, then get someone else to run them so she can go start another."

"What do you like to do?" Though one answer to that was fairly obvious. Nicky was sitting across Kate's ass, massaging her back.

"I don't know. Not that."

Kate wanted to pursue the topic but Nicky's hands distracted her. They hadn't talked after that.

As she did the dishes, she continued to relive the night. Just as she was enjoying a particularly vivid image of Nicky hovering over her, leaning forward slightly, mouth open, eyes closed, the phone rang.

Kate could hear a Pretenders album in the background. "I was just thinking about you."

"I must have gotten the message. Want to have lunch?" Nicky asked.

Kate conjured up and held a picture of Nicky's strong shoulders. "Don't you have to work?"

"Not if you can meet me," Nicky answered.

Lunch didn't last long. Neither woman was hungry. They went back to Nicky's and were making love before they got to the bed. After Nicky came, she pushed Kate's hand away.

"I don't think I can take any more."

"Please, again," said Kate.

Nicky didn't go back to work that afternoon.

That first day was followed by three days of nothing but Nicky. They spent most of their time in bed.

They tried a movie one night but it was boring and Kate had her eyes closed through most of it because Nicky had wonderfully dangerous hands that were never still.

Another night they went dancing. Their dancing, as just about everything else they did, was an extension of their lovemaking. Their arms around each other, they watched the dancers. Kate had her hand on the small of Nicky's back, and Nicky was talking in great detail about the L.A. music scene. And all the time Kate was rubbing her back and Nicky had her hand on Kate's thigh and their legs were touching and Nicky was talking right into Kate's ear, her lips brushing it lightly.

"I hope you didn't expect me to pay any attention to what you were saying," Kate told Nicky later, in bed.

"I didn't. I just liked the way it felt."

"I could've come right there."

Nicky smiled. "That was the point."

Nicky had to go back to work. But this intrusion of the real world hardly slowed them down. They made time to be together. Kate stopped by the store, had lunch with Nicky, picked her up after work. They talked on the phone several times a day.

They didn't talk about their relationship or the future or even the past. (Beyond that first glimpse Nicky had given Kate of Sandy, she hadn't said anything else about her.) They didn't need any other time or frame of reference other than what they created for themselves.

They made love and they went out to eat. Or had extravagant picnics in Nicky's empty living room while they listened to records. Except for those two forays out to the bar and to the movie, they kept to themselves. They didn't need anyone else.

They talked about their friends, "I can't wait till you meet —" or "You'll see what I mean when you meet her." But they never made any plans to get together with anyone.

When Nicky was at work Kate tried to keep herself busy. She went out to the beach, armed with a book and Nicky's Walkman. Dutifully, Kate listened to the tapes Nicky had picked out for her, part of her educational process. They had dissimilar tastes in music but Kate listened because it was like having Nicky around. She tried to read but all she could see was the roundness of Nicky's breast, feel its weight in her hand, or the nipple stiffening under her tongue. Kate tried to think of other things, but kept imagining Nicky's fingers pushing faster and faster inside her.

She lay back in her chair and listened to the music, resigned to fantasizing about what they would do later.

Without even thinking about it Kate brought Nicky home, something she hadn't been able to do with Hilary. She made love with Nicky in almost every room, getting rid of ghosts.

Already things that reminded her of Nicky were taking on special significance. Instead of listening to her usual jazz station, Kate wandered around the dial — rock, soul, Top 40 — searching for songs she associated with Nicky, with dancing with Nicky. An extra awareness had been added to Kate's life, a new neighborhood.

On more than one morning, when she hadn't spent the night with Nicky, she would be waiting with fresh croissants when Nicky came back from her morning run. Kate would make coffee while Nicky showered. Sometimes they made love. Nicky would go off to work and Kate would finish the last crumbs and clean up before leaving.

One afternoon Kate came home to find Nicky's car in the driveway. That was enough to excite her — then Nicky opened the door wearing only a towel.

"Good timing. I just got out of the shower."

Kate slowly moved to Nicky, pulled the towel away and dropped it to the floor. She held Nicky, loved the feeling of her nakedness against her clothes. She moved Nicky backwards into the living room. They kissed. Kate couldn't find one place to keep her hands, they kept moving over Nicky's smooth skin, cupping her ass, stroking her back. Kate kissed Nicky's shoulder, her breast, tongued her nipples. She slowly moved down her body until she was kneeling before Nicky. She took Nicky in her mouth, moved her tongue inside her. Nicky moaned, bent her knees, came closer to Kate. But Kate wouldn't let her lie down until Nicky could no longer stand.

When Nicky came she arched her back, lifting her hips off the carpet. Kate followed, never taking her mouth away.

Nicky bucked and tried to pull away but Kate stayed with her until she came again, calling out Kate's name.

Kate rested her head on Nicky's thigh. "I should have done this that first night we went out. Then we wouldn't have had to waste all that time at dinner."

Time, previously such a burden to Kate, suddenly was light and comfortable. She stopped seeing Hilary and saw only Nicky. They skated at the beach, they drove up to Santa Barbara. Hiked in the Santa Monica mountains. Kate thought maybe they were spending too much time together. After all, where was this leading? But she didn't want to examine things, she had been doing too much of that lately and the close scrutiny bored her. And, if she stopped to think, she might restrain herself.

She knew that she and Nicky had fallen into each other to heal themselves. Sandy and Anne were a part of them. At first. Feeling as much as they did for their ex-lovers, they had a relationship based on these two other women. Strangers to each other, and strangers to the other's ex-, they had an immediate bond. Kate felt reckless and at the same time ·exhilarated. She and Nicky were slamming into each other like bumper cars. They made love with a violence and intensity that surprised her. Then they would sleep in each other's arms, pressed against each other for protection against their dreams.

For as long as possible, Kate put off introducing Nicky to her friends. Because she wasn't ready to venture out into the world again, she told herself. She didn't want to be reminded of what it was like to be part of a couple, didn't want her friends to compare Nicky to Anne, to compare what Kate was like with Nicky to what she'd been like with Anne.

That's what she told herself. But maybe it was really that she knew something was slightly off about the whole situation. Maybe the crazy thing about Nicky was that all along Kate knew that she was being used as a fill-in for Sandy. Or maybe the craziness was that she didn't care.

Kate helped Nicky fight her ghosts with tricks she had learned from her own breakup. When they made love, Kate would keep the light on so that Nicky wouldn't see what was waiting for her in the dark. (Kate remembered not being able to close her eyes because Anne waited for her in the dark. In the dead time between events, everywhere.)

The whole affair had snuck up on her. Kate was surprised at how much she felt for Nicky. (Or was it just that same confusion of sex with intimacy?) And yet Kate couldn't help but notice the gaps, places where she could have said

"I love you." Or would have said it, if she'd been with Anne. They occurred during sex or just after. Close tender moments when the words hung in the air. Or their absence hung in the air.

Kate knew where all the spaces were. They stayed empty. She searched Nicky's eyes, looked hard, trying with her own to communicate something. Now she should have said it. Or now. But she didn't. And was sad, because she couldn't say anything.

Kate envied Nicky her ability to be comfortable in new situations. The first time they had gone to dinner at Jennifer and Eve's house, Nicky had been a great hit with Jennifer's kids. She brought them a bunch of cassettes, groups that Kate hadn't even heard of. But Diane and Allison went wild. Eve and Jennifer had seemed to like her, but Kate suspected that they thought Nicky wasn't "enough" for her. (Though when she asked Jennifer on the phone the next day if that's what she thought, Jennifer had said, "Projection, your honor." And Kate wondered if maybe Jennifer had been right. Maybe that's what she herself suspected.)

Kate didn't like Nicky's friends at all. She was uncomfortable around them. Suddenly nine or ten years made a big difference. Maybe if she hadn't met Amanda first, she would have felt differently.

"Kate, Amanda. Amanda, Kate." Nicky had introduced them proudly. She had already told Kate that Amanda was her closest friend. Kate had no idea what Nicky had told Amanda about her.

Amanda was twenty-four years old and worked in retail. The rag trade. You were either bitten by the bug or not, she confided to Kate.

She also said, "There are certain things I know I want to get done during a day, and by the end of the day, they're done."

Maybe Kate had been jealous of that decisiveness, since it was a trait she definitely lacked. But there was something else about Amanda. She reminded Kate of two young women she had seen in an old Dodge on Melrose Avenue, both with bleached platinum hair, wearing ray bans, smoking and chewing gum, and listening to the radio. They were doing the punk trip to the limit, shocking orange scarves and studded leather wristbands, stark white faces, cheekbones highlighted with brown-red slashes. On closer examination, they were baby-faced girls, no older than seventeen. But they took themselves so seriously, had no sense of humor about the way they were presenting themselves. Here they were in these great get-ups, in the perfect car with the perfect clothes on the perfect Avenue and they were too self-consicous to enjoy it.

Amanda was like that — too studied, too consciously with-it, trying too hard to have a good time. So were a lot of Nicky's other friends. All Kate could see was surface — at least that was all they offered. They reminded her of the women she saw at the bars who were great looking but unapproachable.

And when Nicky was with her friends, she changed. Kate's differences from Nicky were magnified when she was around Nicky's friends. Differences Kate saw repeated in each friend. How alike they all were — and how different from Kate.

Probably, after all of her analyzing of Nicky's friends, what she missed most was the innocent Nicky that she had been drawn to. When they went out with Nicky's friends, Nicky dressed more like them. The current punky-funky style, futuristic clothes with huge shoulder pads and lots of zippers and snaps and flaps. Kate liked Nicky better when Nicky wore her jeans and T-shirt. That was her person, the one she recognized.

Kate started making excuses not to spend time with

Nicky's friends. Until Nicky had finally said, "You know, I can see them without you." It was a solution, not a threat.

Without really talking about it, they went back to their original routine. They pretty much gave up on socializing with friends, preferring to do that on their own time. Nicky would sometimes come home with new records (Kate's collection grew considerably) and they would make dinner together and listen to music. Sometimes Nicky arrived first, and Kate would walk in to music and smells from the kitchen. Nicky was a very unorthodox cook: "Experimental would be putting in mildly," she described it, but the results were usually delicious.

They would spend their evenings listening to records Nicky had found, records Kate had forgotten she owned. As they listened to the old songs, Kate would tell Nicky what she associated with them. She talked about her college days. Dredged up scenes she hadn't thought about in years; less about the student strikes and protests than about finding out she was gay. Making love in a tower room of the library that hardly anyone knew about. Getting stuck in her lover's room during a fire drill, trying to decide if it was really a drill or the real thing, did they have to get out of bed or not. Making excuses for all the time they spent together.

"It seems like such a big deal," Nicky said after hearing of all the intricate deceptions.

"It was, at the time. We didn't know anyone else who was doing anything remotely like that."

"I just fell in love with my best friend in ninth grade and that was that." Nicky was very matter of fact about it all.

Kate wished everything could be so simple.

Kate was invited to Eve and Jennifer's for a grown-ups-only meal. The kids were going to be at a Dodgers game with their father. A black turbo Saab Kate didn't recognize was parked in the driveway, and Kate hoped Eve and Jennifer weren't trying to fix her up with one of their single friends. A quick glance inside the car — she had once considered buying one for herself — revealed that the back seat had been folded down to make room for framed paintings or prints wrapped in blankets. There were also swatches of fabric, and a fan of Dunn-Edwards paint samples. And a very beautiful soup tureen nestled among a wad of towels.

Inside, Eve and Jennifer sat at the dining room table with another woman (as soon as Kate saw her, she thought: I wouldn't mind being set up with her). They were studying plans for an addition to the house.

"We knew we'd never find a house we liked as much as this, so we're adding on," Eve said. "It's about time the kids had their own rooms."

"Kids, hell, you just want a window seat in *our* bedroom. Not to mention a fireplace." Jennifer turned to Kate. "Do you know each other? Lauren's our architectural designer." Jennifer gave the title an extra flourish.

Kate took Lauren's hand. Lauren had a firm handshake, and met Kate's gaze with intense, pale gray-blue eyes, a surprise contrast to her almost black hair.

After the introductions, Lauren, who had begun to gather her plans together, said, "I'll give you room to eat." She was invited to dinner and persuaded to stay.

They had Kate's favorite kind of evening, ranging over all sorts of topics for hours. They spent a long time at the table, lingered over each course, over dessert and coffee.

They talked about the quality of light in New York as compared to Los Angeles. And food. They compared notes on their favorite restaurants.

They agreed and disagreed on issues. They talked about politics and gay politics and women. They talked about writing and art and architecture and being creative under a deadline. Kate was fascinated by Lauren's profession. She knew some of the buildings Lauren had designed, had admired their clean elegance and strong presence.

They were still talking when the kids came home, and were still at it after they'd gone up to bed.

Some time in the course of the evening Kate realized that in the middle of Nicky, in the middle of feeling secure again and happy to be alone, at a time when she'd thought she'd be unable to notice anyone else, she had suddenly seen Lauren. As if Eve and Jennifer hadn't been there and it had been just Lauren, talking to Lauren and learning about Lauren.

This scared Kate a little. Lauren's presence was so solid that Kate felt she could tell her anything, look at her forever. She was a possibility Kate was not willing to explore.

Lauren left before Kate did. They shook hands, Lauren poised and elegant, saying she enjoyed meeting Kate, would look for her name on TV, hoped to see her again.

Kate fumfered, started a lot of sentences, finished none, was grateful at least that she had a firm handshake.

After Lauren was gone, Eve and Jennifer were very obvious in their *not* discussing her with Kate.

Their strategy worked. As much to humor her friends as to satisfy her own curiosity, Kate asked, "How come I've never seen her around?"

Eve answered. "She's been out of circulation about two years. Her lover died in a plane crash."

"Was that who Chris was?" Kate remembered references during dinner, had assumed they referred to a mutual friend. "Had they been together long?"

"Eleven years."

"You might remember her," Jennifer said. "She was a reporter on the evening news."

"Chris *Chandler*?"

Jennifer nodded.

"I remember when that happened." Kate thought about Lauren, tried to imagine what she must have gone through.

"Lauren's only now coming out of it," said Eve.

Kate was now sure that the chance encounter hadn't been chance at all, and said as much to her friends.

To which Jennifer replied: "Right. We're spending all this money to build an addition to our house so you can have a date."

A few days later, preparing to make dinner for Nicky, Kate called her at the store. "Anything you absolutely hate?" She could hear jazz in the background, a piece they had made love to the week before.

"Anchovies. I'll be over around six-thirty."

When Kate hung up, she pulled out several cookbooks for inspiration, decided on a pasta with scallops, followed by salad and cheese. Dessert — well, she figured, when had they ever been able to sit through a meal long enough to get to dessert?

She even enjoyed marketing. It was part of her anticipation of the evening. She drove home smiling, eager to cook for her lover, to make the table beautiful. She stopped on the way and bought bunches of flowers to put all over the house — gladiolas for the living room, iris for the dining table, and her favorite, sweet-smelling freesia for the night table next to the bed.

Dinner was a big success. And she had been right not to plan dessert.

Afterwards, they caught up on the last few days. Kate

told Nicky about the design for Jennifer's house.

Nicky observed ruefully that Kate talked more about the designer than about the design. "She sounds like your kind of person."

"All I said was that I thought it would be interesting to do that kind of work."

"Don't get defensive. All *I* said was she sounded like your kind of person."

"And what are you?"

"Something for in between."

Kate wanted to disagree, protest. She was surprised that Nicky had voiced what she herself had been thinking. But she didn't want to talk about it, though it was obvious that Nicky did.

They really didn't have much in common. And great sex wasn't going to cover up for that indefinitely.

But what was the point of trying to talk with Nicky? They always ended up having sex. It was their only way of communicating.

Kate kept Lauren as a secret for herself, something to pull out and examine when she was alone.

Lying next to Kate, Nicky stretched. "What time is it?"

Kate reached for her watch. "Nine-thirty."

They had turned to each other, very early, around six and made love, then gone back to sleep.

They rolled towards each other and kissed. Kate lay with her head on Nicky's shoulder, a leg thrown over Nicky's body, a hand on the curve of Nicky's hip.

"I must have been a cat in a former life," Kate said sleepily.

"Why is that?" Nicky absently stroked Kate's hair.

"Because I'm purring."

Nicky kissed the top of Kate's head.

They lay awake for a few minutes, Nicky stroking Kate's hair, Kate with her hand between Nicky's legs, Nicky still wet from their lovemaking. Kate fell asleep thinking she wanted to get up and get going but she didn't know where she wanted to go or what it was she wanted to do.

Kate slept for about an hour. A very deep sleep, with no memory of dreaming. It was still cloudy-foggy outside when she woke.

"A perfect day for staying in bed," Kate said as she nuzzled closer to Nicky, stroking her arm.

Nicky responded by kissing Kate's neck, straying down to her breasts. Still half asleep, Kate at first thought to restrain Nicky. But it felt too good. Nicky's hands moved all over her body, stroking, kneading, exploring. She felt between Kate's legs, moved away again.

It started quite lazily. Teasing each other, a few strokes here, kisses here, and here. A tongue darting around a nipple, suggestions of more to come. As Nicky began to make love to her, Kate's mind wandered a little. To their lovemaking of the night before, when Nicky had grabbed her while she was doing the dishes, which reminded her that she had to soak the pot this morning, should have done it last night. A few images of Lauren at dinner floated across, also.

But Kate always came back to Nicky's mouth and hands and the things she was feeling because of them. Nicky lowered her head over Kate and stroked her with her hair. Then she gently pushed Kate's legs apart and bent between them, easing her hands under Kate's ass to raise her to her mouth.

All other thoughts were gone now as Kate watched Nicky between her legs: dark brows, long dark lashes, her eyes closed as she strained to get deeper inside. Then Kate closed her eyes to the most brilliant blues and greens, their intensity changing with the rhythm of Nicky's tongue on her clitoris.

Kate found Nicky's mouth with her hand, felt Nicky's tongue on her fingers, sucking her in. The closer Kate came to orgasm, the more excited Nicky became. With Nicky's tongue on her, Nicky's fingers inside her, Kate pushed against her lover's mouth, ready to come, right on the edge before falling over. But Nicky surprised her by pulling away. She would make Kate wait.

Kate sat up, wanting Nicky in her mouth. But Nicky buried herself deeper between Kate's legs, not teasing now, sucking at her with an intensity that shut everything else out of Kate's mind.

Until: "Do you want to get that?"

Apparently the phone had rung.

"No," said Kate as she reached for Nicky. The moment had been lost, but it would not take much to find it again.

Nicky had sat up when the phone rang. Now Kate pulled her back down, turning her around so that Nicky was stretched out on top of her, her back against Kate's front.

Kate kissed Nicky's shoulder while her hands moved over Nicky's breasts and stomach. She spread Nicky's legs open with her own, caressed her thighs. She could feel Nicky's buttocks against her.

"I'm so close," said Nicky.

"Wait," whispered Kate, "together."

Kate rubbed her fingers over Nicky's clitoris, sometimes sliding inside her. They moved together, Nicky pressing down into Kate, Kate straining upwards against Nicky. "Oh God," one of them said. Or both. Nicky reached down and touched Kate. Each moved faster and faster. Then they were coming, shaking the bed and the room with their movement and their cries.

They lay together, out of breath, Nicky still draped over Kate.

"Am I too heavy?"

Kate held her. "Not at all." Then, "Jesus."

They smiled, proud of themselves.

This time when the phone rang, Kate answered it, waiting with her hand on the receiver for one more ring to gain another few seconds to pull herself together. Nicky lay next to her, stroking Kate's hip as she talked on the phone. Kate mouthed "my father" to her.

Still wrapped up in the lovemaking, she couldn't see straight, much less talk. Some old version of herself tried to clean herself up as she talked to him. She remembered necking on dates when she was in school; hearing her parents' keys in the door and jumping off the couch and into a chair, whichever boyfriend she was with hastily fixing his shirt, his tie, sometimes his zipper (though that was when she was a little older). Of course their hair was all messed up, cheeks pink, eyes bright, lips red. Her father, after whoever had left, would zing her a line like, "Tom looked neater the last time I saw him." Kate looked back now and could smile at his teasing. She hadn't been able to then.

Today, her father started off with preliminaries: How are you, how's the weather, any word on when they'd start production. And all the while Nicky teased her, wouldn't stop touching her, kissed her back, her breasts.

"When did you find out?" Kate didn't have to push Nicky away; Nicky had already stopped, apparently hearing something in Kate's voice.

Kate listened. "When?" Pause. "For how long?"

Not knowing what was going on, Nicky took Kate's hand and held it, trying to comfort her, but Kate was oblivious. Two minutes ago all she had been aware of was her body and now she was completely disconnected from it. Nicky watched her face in obvious concern.

"I'll leave as soon as I can. I'll call you after I've seen her."

After she hung up, Kate didn't say anything. Nicky didn't push her, but waited anxiously for an explanation.

Finally: "I'm going to go to New York. My great-aunt is going into the hospital for chemotherapy."

Kate turned on the shower as hot as she could bear and stood under the jet, lowering her head to let the water hit her neck.

She was trying to wash away the last few days: the memories of Nicky in her mouth; the surprising need she had to be held by this woman, to be both inside and outside her.

Even now, after the sobering call from her father, she felt a shiver of excitement when she thought about making love to Nicky. Putting her hand between Nicky's legs to find her already wet. No matter how many times, no matter how many women, this was always new.

"Alice's cancer is back." That's what her father said.

Alice's liver cancer had been diagnosed over a year ago. Some part of Kate had been waiting for this phone call. She appreciated his trying to break the news as simply as possible.

A mirror image of events that were sixteen years old, when he told Kate that her mother had cancer. "They found a little cancer," was all he had said then. Her mother hadn't gone to a doctor until it was too late.

Kate never had a chance to ask why she waited. Never really had a chance to say a proper goodbye to her mother. Kate hadn't been allowed to participate in her mother's death.

To this day she felt cheated. She realized her mother had been protecting her, but she had been nineteen years old, hadn't wanted that kind of protection.

She remembered waiting in the hospital to see her mother after surgery. And Alice, a retired pediatrician, explaining, at least medically, what was happening. Translating for

Kate and her father.

But what was happening in the hospital couldn't be explained. The only thing at the time that had made any sense to Kate were stories about her mother's childhood, stories she heard from Alice. She could recognize her mother in the impetuous and precocious child of the stories but not in the suffering woman in the hospital bed.

And now, sixteen years later, Kate realized that Alice was her last link to her mother.

She started crying in the shower, sobbing so loudly that Nicky rushed in from the other room. Kate couldn't come out and Nicky couldn't comfort her through the sliding glass doors so she climbed in with Kate and held her.

Kate kept crying "I'm sorry, I'm sorry" to Nicky, who held her and kissed her face and tried to comfort her while the water splattered around them and Kate's sobs echoed in the tiled stall.

They stayed there until the hot water started to run out. Then Nicky dried Kate off, put her back to bed, sat next to her, and gently rubbed her back until she was quiet.

Kate made her plane reservations, dropped off an extra set of keys at Jennifer's. She went to the cleaners, cancelled her newspaper, paid some bills. She notified her agent where she would be.

She called her father to tell him when she'd be arriving. Now that the shock had worn off, she could ask questions that hadn't come up when he first told her about Alice.

Apparently, he'd known about Alice's worsening condition for a long time. "We did her will for her a while ago. But now she's going into her bequests in even greater detail. She's dividing everything up. In fact, she wanted me to ask if you wanted those plates you bought for her in Italy."

"Oh God. That must be weird."

What Kate really wanted to know was why she hadn't been told before.

"No one was."

"You were."

"And I was asked not to say anything. I had to respect that." Patiently, as if he were talking to a client who couldn't be expected to understand what was going on.

Her father had always been like that with her, so that business and law, anything that even slightly smacked of either, was a foreign language to Kate. She could deal only in feelings. Compensation, perhaps, for all those years of dealing with a corporate lawyer.

Kate was silent for a long time. This had to be hard on her father, too. After he'd proposed to Kate's mother, Alice had championed his cause to the rest of her family. Who hadn't thought he'd amount to much. Alice had even lent him money when he was first starting out in practice.

"This must be hard on you, Dad."

"You know how these things are." Then, always ready to change the subject, "How are you?"

"Fine, Dad."

"How are you doing about, you know."

"About Anne?"

"Yes."

Kate had to smile. Her father was very supportive of her, always had been. Even though she knew he would rather she hadn't turned out gay. He loved her, that was the important part, and had said from the start that he only wanted her to be happy. And when he saw that she was happy, or rather when he really believed that she was happy, he admitted to himself that this "phase" was not going to go away. She knew that he wanted to be able to talk more openly, but he simply didn't know how.

"I'm fine. Anne's living in New York now, you know."

"You told me."

"That's right."

He had asked — that was enough. They wouldn't talk about it anymore. "I wish we could be here when you came in." He and his second wife, Helen, were going to the Bahamas on vacation.

"I do, too. But you haven't been away in such a long time. I'll see you when you get back. Maybe you'll come out to Palm Springs."

"Maybe."

The last thing he'd said to her was, "Take care of Alice." Kate promised she would.

She had almost finished packing. Nicky had gone out to get them something to eat. They'd had a fight before she left, because Nicky had wanted to talk about their relationship. "I think it might be nice to get some things straight before you go away."

"Too late for that," had been Kate's flip reply. "The straight part, that's what I meant."

"I'm serious," Nicky said. "I know how hard this trip is going to be for you, but I really want us to talk."

"What do you want to talk about? What's there to say? We're doing what we're doing and that's that!"

Nicky tried to calm her, but Kate stayed all ridges and sharp edges — Keep Out.

When Nicky came back with a pizza and some beer, Kate apologized. "I just can't think about anything else right now."

Nicky shrugged her off. "It's understandable."

"Besides," Kate couldn't resist adding, "we're fine. There's nothing to talk about."

But they both knew that wasn't true.

They ate quickly, and Kate went back to her packing. Nicky had brought a small cassette deck into the bedroom.

She put on the Bill Evans tape they had listened to their first night together. She went over to Kate, took her arm. "Leave this," she said.

They went to bed. Kate did everything very slowly. This was saying goodbye. She tried to stay with what was happening, with what she could see and taste and touch. She burrowed deeper into Nicky for protection, asked to be held forever. She guided Nicky's fingers inside herself.

Kate ran her tongue along the ridge of Nicky's spine while Nicky's hands explored her body. She moved between Nicky's legs. At the point where there seemed to be no entrance, that's where she entered and her fingers disappeared.

And then Nicky turned Kate onto her stomach and kissed her back and her legs, stretched out on top of her. Kate kept trying to remember something but kept losing it — no matter, because something at her center anchored her. Kept her pushing against Nicky, tightening her muscles around Nicky's fingers.

When she came, she had the kind of orgasm that was accompanied by insight. A situation seen clearly. Kate hadn't wanted that. Had wanted only the release. Instead: this is going to be the last time.

Nicky clung to Kate, and her coming was the deepest Kate had pulled from her, a low shaking cry that was both celebration and mourning.

They held each other gently after that.

That night Kate dreamt she was in her parent's apartment in New York. It was now, the present, but her mother was still alive. She was out of the apartment but had left a page of notes for Kate.

Kate read the notes but couldn't understand them. That her mother was alive was a given: Kate had only to decipher the notes and she would find her. Maybe Alice would be able to help her.

Kate woke up thinking that the helpless frustration of her dream was how she had felt sometimes in her waking life, that her mother was alive somewhere and that she just hadn't seen her in a very long time.

Like Anne.

Like Alice.

Kate lay in bed for a long time before slipping quietly out of bed to finish packing.

Because they both hated goodbyes, Nicky dropped Kate at the airport.

The flight was crowded, but Kate was lucky: no one sat next to her. She spread her jacket, her book and magazines out on the empty seat and closed herself off from the rest of the passengers. She thought about Nicky. The kiss at the airport had been a goodbye. A rehearsal for goodbye. And on this flight Kate rehearsed the goodbye she would have to say to Alice.

The plane hit some turbulence around Chicago. Kate buckled her seat belt. The closer she got to New York, the more L.A. became a dream. And today Nicky faded away, and the three women waiting for her in New York — Alice, her mother, Anne — loomed larger.

Anne hadn't stood in front of her thoughts until the initial shock of her father's call had worn off. But she was there now, would be waiting at every entrance to the city, waiting for Kate at the end of every block.

"You don't have to call her if it's going to bother you that much," had been Jennifer's advice.

"I don't know if I can let it go like that."

"Well, don't worry about it until you get there."

When the flight attendant announced their final descent into JFK, Kate took a deep breath and fastened her seat belt, trying to ignore the symbolism of a bumpy ride.

PART II

In the cab into the city Kate thought about how California disappeared when she went to New York. Almost as if she had never been there. Whole chunks of her life were gone.

Her driver cursed the five o'clock traffic into Manhattan, but the slow pace enabled Kate to study the view from the 59th Street bridge: a more dense cluster of buildings in midtown than when she was growing up, but the feeling was the same.

In her old neighborhood everything looked small, familiar. Certain buildings and views in her memory were gone, little local stores that had been replaced by big apartment buildings. But these few blocks near her father's were somehow always the same. The buildings seemed smaller and closer together than buildings on other blocks, their familiarity scaling them down to below size.

(When she was thirteen, she returned from a summer trip with her parents and when she saw the clouds in the clear sky she had been so full of the city she had to tell her mother how good it was to be back, how much she loved New York. Her mother had touched her hair, and the touch felt the same as a kiss of congratulation, of complicity. They had the city in common.)

She was always amazed at being so intimately connected to/with the city. After ten years she still had vivid flashes of a particular corner — not just buildings or the quality of the light — but a vignette complete with characters and action. Sometimes it was the corner of 55th and Fifth. The door-man of the St. Regis getting someone a taxi as out-of-town guests left the hotel and stood under the awning trying to figure out which way to walk, east or west. Chauffeurs talk-ing to each other, standing near their limos, a silver stretch-Lincoln and a navy Cadillac. Shoppers and delivery boys hurrying by. Sometimes there would be such a crowd of pedestrians that a car stopped for the light would be swallowed by the crowd, unable to move.

Kate couldn't really say she imagined this scene and others like it. She felt more like she was there, walking through it. And then, of course, when she was really there, on one of her trips to New York, it was like walking through a déjà vu.

Now, though, the changes were more obvious. Nothing was finished, there was too much construction. She marked the differences — buildings not completed on her last trip now fully rented, doormen tipping their hats to residents, chatting and gossiping as if everyone had been there for-ever.

She let herself into her father's apartment. Her father's and *Helen's* apartment, she reminded herself.

Helen had left her a note. "Welcome. Sheets are clean, so are towels in the bathroom. Come back soon so we can visit." To which her father had added "Love you, XXX, Daddy."

Kate put her bags down and walked around. She was amazed at the smell of the apartment, so familiar to her still. Some places never leave you, she thought. No matter how many changes they went through, they felt the same. She stood in the doorway and looked into the room her father shared with Helen. Her parents' room, though it had been years since she'd called it that.

She remembered going in after her parents had gone out.

As soon as she'd hear the elevator door close, meaning they were really gone, she would run into their room to catch their presence still in the air. The light on the dresser would be on, her mother's powdery-perfumy smell on one side of the room mixing with her father's aftershave on the other. The air would still be a little damp from their showers. The rush of their preparations could be felt long after they'd left the house.

Some nights, Kate would hear them when they came home. Then the apartment would feel full again, and she could sleep.

The apartment hadn't felt the same since her mother died. For the first few years after the death the place was depressing. Kate's father hadn't been able to make any changes in the rooms. Once he started going out with Helen, and then after she moved in, things got better; he allowed her to make changes. The rooms seemed strange to Kate. Not that she minded the new couches or the new colors, she welcomed them. But the apartment still had the same smell, the same air. So much was familiar even now, with her mother long gone. As if she hadn't given her father's presence any credit when she was growing up, or even in her memories. It was her mother who had lent her particular atmosphere to the rooms. *Her* presence that had lingered. Being in the old apartment was like being in the city: home but not home. Familiar and unknown.

She went to unpack. She stayed in what used to be her

room. It had been made into a guest room/den/catch all right after Kate had found her first New York apartment. She hadn't lived in it for years, but some of her books were still there, as well as a few boxes in the closet that hadn't been inspected since she first moved out — clearly things she could live without — old college notebooks and letters and even checkbooks from accounts closed for years.

She called Alice and offered to take her to the hospital the next day, but Alice had already arranged that with a friend. "Okay, I'll just meet you there." No mention of cancer or chemotherapy or fear. As casual as arranging tea at the Plaza. Were they pretending? Or was discussion unnecessary?

Kate looked up Anne's number (having to do that felt strange to her) but didn't call.

She felt the beginnings of a headache: the pulling around her jaws, the tightness around her eyes. After she put her things away she took a shower.

Around six she went for a walk. People were still coming home from work. This had always been one of her favorite times. An hour filled with expectations.

Again déjà vu. She would stand next to someone waiting for the light to change. Cars stuck between streets, horns blaring. Everyone hurrying. Crowds swallowing a cab stuck at a light, surging into its wake as it crossed the intersection. It was a specific memory Kate had, renewed each time she went back. Always the same, always the same stuff in the air. The city's energy was visible, especially at this hour. Grab a bite and then hurry to the theatre. Even when she had lived there she hadn't taken the city for granted.

She loved it in summer, when people hurried home to change before going to an outdoor concert, a movie, to find some relief not just from the heat but from the wall of humidity. The thick damp air — she even missed that sometimes.

This hour did not have the same effect on her in L.A., with everyone crowded onto the freeways. It only made her long for New York.

Whenever she came back she found it impossible to believe that she no longer lived in the city. Or she believed it but was in a strange suspension. And she realized she was incorrect in thinking that L.A. disappeared for her. Just that this city could never be anything but home.

She walked around for about an hour, checking on certain of her favorite landmarks. The Lever Brothers building. Once, on the first snow of the season, she and her mother had walked there to see the carousel installed in the lobby every Christmas. The streets were empty that Tuesday night, and very quiet because of the snow. Kate, about eight at the time, never went out on a school night. And never alone with her mother. But that night it had been just the two of them and the city and the pinkish gray sky that meant snow.

It was hard to keep the image of that peace now, the streets were so busy. On the way home Kate stopped at the deli across the street from the apartment.

This was the kind of place that really made her miss New York when she was in L.A. On earlier trips she had tried not going in there, because reminders of countless dinners and lunches and late-night runs for ice cream had been almost more than she could bear.

She still called it Fischer's, though it had changed names even before she moved to L.A. The place itself never changed. The only thing they'd done in the last ten years was to add a refrigerator for cold drinks at the front of the store, near the door.

The place smelled the same. It looked the same. The food tasted the same. The men behind the counter changed, but only every few years, and gradually — a few new faces appearing before an old one left, so that you always recognized at least one of them.

Another constant: something about the way these men handled small objects had always intrigued her. Not so much when they made a sandwich — though she did admire their economy of movement — but the way they put sundries, a pack of cigarettes, a small jar of olives, into a bag, their big beefy hands suddenly delicate and careful.

(The only other inspiration for these feelings came from New York cabbies, hands on their thin steering wheels, taking her wherever with that same economy of motion. Completely familiar with their cars, the streets, the traffic. Accelerating through narrow spaces, knowing exactly the width of their cabs.)

When Kate got back to the apartment she ate her sandwich in silence; no TV, music, magazine or book for company. She thought of Nicky. Not for the first time since they'd parted at the airport. But for the first time with a sense of detachment. It was the silence that did it. Not a still silence — she was, after all, in the heart of mid-town Manhattan. What she noticed was the lack of music. There had never been any quiet with Nicky.

Even though Kate stayed up late reading, she had trouble sleeping. She woke once during the night, disoriented. At first she thought she was in L.A. But then she recognized the rumble of a truck on First Avenue as just that, and not an earthquake. She found she was no longer accustomed to the sounds of the city: the horns and sirens, the constant rumble and clatter of trucks. They crowded into the noises of her dreams.

She woke early and stayed in bed until eight.

She made toast and coffee. She tried Anne around nine, got the machine and hung up. Kate heard Anne's voice saying "we" weren't home. That "we" made her wince. (Though what had she expected, separate phones?) She was disappointed and relieved.

She called her friend Sarah, one of the few people she'd kept in touch with since college, and one of the only friends she wanted to talk to this trip. They decided to meet for a drink after Kate's visit at the hospital. Sarah offered Kate sympathy and encouragement, then Kate was alone with her city.

The day was beautiful. A fine welcome for her, she thought as she got out into it. Bright and clear, everything sharply defined against the sky. She thought of her conversation with Lauren about the light in L.A., its different quality — filtered, never crisp. Lauren had said that the sun's rays had to bounce off millions of particles of smog in the air before finally hitting the trees and buildings. Even a clear day wasn't as clear as New York.

She got to the hospital a little after four. Alice was already in the admitting office filling out forms. Kate stood and watched. She hadn't seen Alice in a long time and wanted a chance to secretly inspect her, to not be surprised by any changes, visible or otherwise, in her aunt.

She appeared to be the same Alice, alert and spunky. (Kate couldn't see Helen Hayes without thinking of Alice. They looked alike — gray hair pulled back from the same bright, round face, all smile and light. She wondered if Helen Hayes had the same jaunty walk, body rocking slightly from side to side.) Alice looked strong and healthy. Though she had lost one eye to the cancer a year ago, the other was still bright. Her hands shook a little. That was new.

When Alice finished with the forms, Kate knocked on the doorframe. The hospital worker looked up before Alice did. "May I help you?"

Kate indicated that she was there to see Alice, who at that moment raised her head. For a split second, still involved in her forms and her cancer, even though she was looking at Kate, Alice seemed afraid and disoriented. Kate wanted to run to her. Instead, Alice recovered quickly and spoke first, "Oh Kate, darling, how good to see you!" She turned to the hospital worker, "My favorite niece. All the way from California."

"How nice."

Kate went with her to the vault. The woman there, Theodora McNulty according to her name tag, took the credit cards Alice gave her, plus twenty-five dollars in cash. Alice wanted to keep seven dollars for herself. But McNulty said "Keep only two, it's safer that way." She persuaded Alice to give her the stone-studded gold ring she always wore. Alice had bought the ring in Thailand (then Siam) thirty years earlier. But Alice drew the line at her watch.

"No, I can't give you that. I need that."

And McNulty finally had to give up. Alice said, in a matter-of-fact tone that seemed to be directed to herself, "A watch is important, you need a watch." But Kate suspected she was also thinking, "What's a doctor without a watch?"

"I'd rather be a doctor than a patient," Alice confided to Kate as she watched Theodora McNulty lock her possessions in the vault.

"I'd rather be a writer than either," Kate said.

Small jokes seemed even less funny when offered in a small hospital office. Kate looked around for a box of Kleenex, put a tissue in her pocket for later. Just in case.

Alice's friend Catherine had driven her to the hospital. She returned from parking the car just as Kate and Alice were on their way upstairs. The three went to Alice's room.

Kate loved watching them together. Both so deaf (and this was another change Kate added to her list: Alice's hearing was worse than ever) they were always repeating everything in English and German, back and forth. Alice couldn't always hear Kate when she spoke to her, but when a coat fell off the dresser onto the floor, *tck,* one of its buttons hitting the floor, "What was that?" she wanted to know.

"Your coat fell on the floor," Kate said as she stooped to pick it up. "I'm going to hang it on the back of the door."

"What?"

A little louder: "The button hit the floor when your coat fell."

"What?"

"YOUR COAT. IT FELL."

"Why don't you hang it up?"

The next project was a photograph. Kate had bought a small fully automatic camera for this trip; she intended to use it as she would a note pad. Also, she knew Alice, an amateur photographer, loved gadgets and would be intrigued with this one. But posing Alice and Catherine was no easy production.

"You sit in the chair, I'll sit on the arm." Catherine wanted Alice to be comfortable.

"No, you."

"No, sit."

"No, you sit here."

"No, Alice. . . ."

"No, you sit, I'll sit on the arm, you're taller than I am."

Once the truth came out, that Alice was a little embarrassed about her height, the argument was settled. Kate had let them fight it out because making herself heard was too tiring. She just waited until they were done.

She stayed only a few minutes after taking the photos. Having a bit of time until she had to meet Sarah, she walked through the Park, stopping every so often to take a look around, mark her place. Letting the city comfort her.

Already the hospital was getting to her. And though Alice had looked fine, and in pretty good shape, Kate could tell she was nervous and afraid. Alice's condition brought back familiar (familiar even after sixteen years) feelings that she'd experienced when her mother was sick. Fear, frustration, helplessness. It had been easy to be in L.A. and say, "I'm going to New York to see my aunt in the hospital." Easy enough to clear the decks for the trip. Harder to imagine the impact of actually being there.

Every time she passed a phone booth on the way to the Plaza she had to resist the temptation to call Anne.

Kate was supposed to meet Sarah at the Oak Bar around 5:30. Sarah, a producer for public television, was always late, so Kate wasn't surprised to see her pushing through the line at 5:45.

They hugged, Sarah not even taking time to put down any of the three bags she always carried — one purse and two canvas bags containing scripts and papers and contracts and God knew what else. She barely took time to breathe between sentences. "Fifteen minutes, not bad for me! I thought you'd be at a table or on your fifth drink by now. How's your aunt? You look wonderful."

"So do you."

Sarah ran her fingers through her blond hair. "Do you like it better without the perm? I can't decide whether or not to have it done again."

They had to wait for a table. The room was full of tourists and businessmen and people who looked as if they were having affairs. The couple in front of them moved to a table near the bar.

"Good," Kate said. "Now we'll get that table by the window."

The windows were the reason Kate liked the Oak Bar. Very large clear panes of glass fronting 59th Street, Central Park South. She could see the tops of horse-drawn carriages, and the tips of trees in the park across the street. She liked coming here because she could imagine an older New York, New York of the Twenties, or Thirties or Forties. How elegant to be having a drink here in those days. (But then, in those days, women were not allowed in the Oak Bar. Kate figured there would always be trade-offs.)

During her last few years in New York she had spent much time in search of the old city. She read about its history, its landmarks, plus any old novels she could find that were set in New York. She loved reading about it in Henry James, or Edith Wharton. She went for tea at the Algonquin, the Waldorf, or the Plaza, did everything she could think of to steep herself in the city's past. Anything to contrast with the overwhelming feeling of the new New York, The Big Apple, the one that felt like New York Magazine or "Bloomies": trendy, but not real; some ad agency's idea of the city.

"I think I might have a baby."

Kate, brought abruptly back to New York of the 1980s, looked at Sarah, who was staring at her, waiting for a reaction.

When none was forthcoming, Sarah asked, "What do you think?"

"Are you getting married?"

"I didn't think you'd be so conventional."

"It's not so much the marriage part that I was concerned with. Do you have someone in mind for the father?"

"Maybe."

"Does he know?"

"I'm not sure I want to tell him."

"Oh boy."

Kate knew this was going to be a good evening. She could always count on Sarah for something interesting. Once, when they had been shopping, in the middle of Zabar's cheese section Sarah had announced to Kate, "My therapist says I'm not gay." Kate, although she almost dropped the stilton she'd picked up, hadn't said anything. She knew there'd be more. And sure enough: "She said I was just highly eroticized."

It turned out that Sarah had been going through a sort of sexual identity crisis — "Well, most of my best friends, male and female, are gay. What'd you expect?" After a terrible history of relationships with men, she had figured she'd be better off with women. Being with women hadn't made her happy, either. (Which was pretty much what Kate had expected.) So Sarah had gone back to men, always finding one but, at least according to her, never the right one.

"So who do you have in mind for the father?"

"I don't even know if I've gotten that far yet. I know I want to raise a child, and I'm getting to the point of no return, agewise."

They spent the rest of the evening talking about children and relationships. The question of having or not having children was one that Kate hadn't yet settled for herself, so she took the subject very seriously. She was answering Sarah's questions as well as her own, hoping to discern how she felt about the issue at the same time. She had had the same conversation with a lot of her friends in L.A. Both Eve and Jennifer encouraged her toward motherhood, no matter how she accomplished the objective. Kate wasn't sure yet. She had a few years to think about it still. And, she didn't want to raise a child alone.

Kate didn't get back to the apartment until two. She and Sarah hadn't solved anybody's problems, but they had talked about them all. She had even told Sarah a little about Lauren. Exhausted, Kate crawled into bed. She had been able to forget, if only for a little while, why she was here. That night she was lulled to sleep by the traffic noise.

* * * * *

Alice was nervous before her first treatment.

"I'll stay here and keep you company," Kate offered.

"No, dear, I'll be fine. You go for a little walk."

Kate didn't know how long the chemotherapy would take. Not knowing what else to do, she walked around the main floor of the hospital for a half hour or so, until she thought it was safe to go back to the room.

Alice received two injections, the first an anti-nausea drug (Kate thought she heard someone say it was Thorazine) to counteract the effect of the second. After that day, Alice changed her mind about Kate's being in the room.

A routine became established. When Kate first arrived, Alice would be very lively and happy to see her, chattering to her about something she had read in the morning papers. For most hospital inconveniences — having her blood pressure or temperature taken, having blood drawn — Alice could assume a certain detached interest in her own case. (A professional distance that reminded Kate of her father.)

But all pretense at maintaining that distance collapsed as the time drew closer for her doctor to give her her shot. Growing increasingly anxious, she would lie on the bed, very tense, usually closing her eyes, closing her face tight. Kate would look out the window for what seemed hours (it must have seemed much longer to Alice).

Kate didn't like being in the room for the shots. She stayed partly because she knew it helped Alice and partly because she hated walking in the halls.

Being here with Alice was much harder than she'd imagined. There was an unreality about the situation. Similar to being in New York. She was removed from something that was supposed to be home. And yet everything reminded her of something she'd gone through when her mother had been sick, something she'd seen or heard. She was caught in a time warp. This was happening now, this had happened then, then was a long time ago but she remembered it so vividly, how long ago could it have been?

Kate's mother had been in another hospital, in a room at the end of a corridor. Back then, as soon as Kate pushed open the doors to that corridor, she would hear a woman moaning in pain. A constant sound. No one was ever in the room with that woman, and she never kept quiet. And as Kate walked down the hall to her mother's room, she found herself marching in step with that other woman's pain.

And then she would see her mother. In a big sunny room with an I.V. in her arm and pain everywhere. When Kate came down from school to visit, she couldn't leave the hospital, even after she had physically left the hosptial. Riding back on the train, when they came out of the tunnel under Park Avenue, she could see the hospital from the window. It followed her until the tracks curved away from the city.

New York felt like two cities this trip. One was the place that made her feel good, that had always given her strength, excited her. The other was the city she remembered from when her mother was sick. The place that disappeared to make room for the hospital.

After the first day, the days all ran together, all the days alike: when she wasn't at the hospital, a lot of walking, visiting favorite places. Kate knew all the details of her trip, what she had done, but she couldn't remember when — the first day or the fifth, after the first chemotherapy treatment or the third.

And no matter what she did or whom she was with, she was always aware of Alice in the hospital. Waiting. Waiting for the night to be over. Waiting for the first nurse with breakfast or medication. Waiting for visitors to come. For them to leave. Waiting for the shot to prevent the nausea caused by the chemotherapy. Waiting for the chemotherapy. Waiting for the night.

And no matter where Kate was she felt connected to the

hospital. It became a new center of the city, raised on the map in her head.

It was so easy to fall into hospital routine. Making small talk. Or sometimes just sitting. Once Kate watched Alice stare out the window. It was a gray rainy day, though the weather had little effect on the city and business was going on as usual. The scenes outside the window looked like the background for Alice's thoughts.

Alice kept up a cheerful front except when alone with Kate. One day two of Alice's other great-nieces visited and stayed for hours. "They stayed too long," Alice said when they had left.

"You should have asked them to leave sooner."

Alice shrugged. "They only wanted to be nice." She sighed. "I'm so tired."

And she and Kate sat comfortably in silence.

Alice seemed grateful to be allowed to rest, to be silent. Sometimes they talked. Once in awhile about death. But usually about whatever: old memories, silly things. Sometimes Alice confused Kate with Kate's mother. Which one had shown her her first gray hairs? Kate reminded her that they both had. Alice sometimes talked to Kate in German, slipping in and out of the language, as if she were talking to Kate's mother.

They were thinking parallel thoughts, both spending time with the same woman: Alice with her niece, Kate with her mother.

She didn't speak to Anne until several days after she'd arrived.

She had just gotten out of the shower when the phone rang. She figured it was Sarah; they had a seven o'clock dinner date, and this time she was the one running behind schedule. She dashed across the room to get the phone.

"I know, I know. I'm late."

"I wouldn't recognize you if you were on time."

Kate froze. She held her towel more tightly against her chest. "Anne."

"I got your message. I didn't know you were coming to town. Can we get together?"

Oh God, thought Kate. It had been her own idea to call, yet suddenly she found herself frantically coming up with excuses for not seeing Anne.

"How are you?" Kate stalled. "You sound good." I don't, thought Kate. Too tentative.

"I feel pretty good. I'd forgotten how much I liked living here. And I love my new job."

Yeah, and we're fucking our brains out all the time. This is the best relationship I've ever been in. Kate couldn't help but add her own version of Anne's thoughts. Stay out of there, she warned herself. But she knew she wouldn't be able to listen to that voice. She could hardly listen to Anne's. Though she kept trying to tell herself that that was because Anne was babbling about *stuff*, nothing real, nothing important, just. . . . Well, just whatever you would talk about to someone who once was everything to you and who now is not only nothing but not even a nearby nothing. Now they were "just friends." And Anne had someone else to talk to.

Kate had heard a radio talk show shrink in San Francisco once. Some guy had called in, still depressed about a three-year relationship that had ended a year earlier. He went on and on about how miserable he felt, "I'm depressed all the time, I can't go out, I don't want to meet new people." A litany of despair. And the therapist had cut him off. "Paul, is it over?" And Paul had said yes, then continued his litany. "Paul, is it over?" "Yes." "Is a table a table?" "Yes." "Is it over, Paul?" "Yes."

It seemed awfully simple to Kate, "Is a table a table?" But she liked it, it had a nice ring. The question became kind of a password for her.

And as Anne went on about whatever, Kate kept asking herself over and over again whether or not a table was, in fact, a table.

"What did you say?"

It wasn't until Anne asked that, her voice puzzled, that Kate realized she must have asked her question out loud. "Nothing. Sorry, go on."

"You sound kind of distracted."

"I don't know why I would." Kate had hoped she could keep the sarcasm out of her voice.

"Look, this isn't easy for either of us."

"Why should it be hard for you?"

There was a long silence at the other end. Kate knew she'd hurt Anne a little with that, wished she didn't feel kind of glad about it. A cheap shot. Anne had had her own reasons for leaving, and at least things hadn't gotten all drawn out like some other crumbled relationships Kate had seen. Even though it was nice to know that she still had some effect on Anne, Kate wanted to make amends for the snide remark.

"At least this isn't long distance." Kate wasn't sure her attempt at humor would be appreciated. The continued silence confirmed that it wasn't. "Hey, I was just trying for a little comic relief."

"I know."

"How come you know everything now and you didn't know everything then?" How come I can't shut up, Kate added to herself.

"We've already had this conversation, I think."

"And every other one in the book."

" 'The book of love, uh, love, uh, la, la, la-la-la *love,*' "

Anne sang.

"Very funny," but without sarcasm.

"Now, are you going to tell me why you're here?"

"Alice is in the hospital."

How much easier to talk to someone who knew her history. She told Anne about the hospital, her visits with Alice, how everything reminded her of her mother. And then she started to cry. But this time she couldn't control it. "I'm sorry, I didn't want to do this."

"Oh honey, what can I do?"

"Nothing. Just. . . . Nothing."

After all the months of pushing Anne out of her head, out of her life, here she was, a matter of life and death, and Anne was all she wanted. It didn't matter that Anne was not available. This was what she wanted. She needed that familiarity now, that's what she'd needed all week. Someone to cry to. Nicky had tried to help, but couldn't come in deep enough. Sarah couldn't do it for her, nor could any of her other friends. Only Anne. There had been times during the week, as she walked around the city, as she sat by Alice's bed, went up in the elevator to the room, when she would have given anything to hold Anne's hand close to her heart. Just for five seconds. Or just to have her there. Just five minutes alone with her, without anything else, without the breakup. No promises, just Anne's hand close to her heart.

And here she was.

The shock of that realization surprised her. What she wanted seemed very clear right now, funny that she hadn't realized it sooner. She still wanted Anne, and maybe they had a chance, maybe they could get together. . . .

Kate heard something from Anne's end of the line, someone in the background.

"Jane just got home, can you hold on a second?" And then muffled sounds because Anne put her hand over the receiver while they did whatever they did when Jane just got home.

And Kate remembered where she was and why and took back a little of herself. How quick she was to give it away. Anne had been a part of her. And when Anne left, Kate had felt an empty space inside. She had started to fill it, without even realizing that that's what she'd been doing, and, though the hole remained, it no longer had Anne's outline, so that even if Anne came back, she wouldn't fit. It had taken months to learn that, and she had forgotten in just a few seconds. She would have to keep an eye on herself with Anne.

"Sorry about that." Anne was back on the line.

"That's okay." Well, here goes. Kate closed her eyes and took the plunge. "Do you have any time over the weekend?"

"Are you sure you want to see me?"

"No, I'm not sure, for Christ's sake, but I though maybe we could try."

"Okay."

"Sunday brunch?" Jerk, thought Kate, of course not Sunday brunch. She's got Jane. Why are you putting her through this? If you lived with someone you'd want to spend Sunday with her, not go see your whiny ex-lover. "Or how about breakfast tomorrow?"

"That's a little better for me."

Sure, so you can stay in bed with Jane. Stop, Kate told herself. Is a table a table? Leave her alone.

So they made plans to meet in the Village the next morning.

Kate hung up feeling medium about the call. She wished she could let up just a little bit. Not that Anne didn't deserve a little trouble, but what was the point? Kate was the one who became upset. Before she could finish dressing, the phone rang again. This time it *was* Sarah, and Kate, by now very, very late for dinner, apologized.

"I was talking to Anne."

Silence from Sarah, who was not usually at a loss for words. "I was trying to think of something clever to say, but I'll just ask how you're doing."

"Okay. I guess."

"You still want to have dinner, don't you?"

"More than ever."

Kate and Sarah ate at one of Kate's favorite restaurants, a small neighborhood steak house that she liked not so much because of the food (though that was fine, very simply prepared), but because she couldn't find anything like it in L.A. All dark wood and polished brass. The same family had owned and operated it since the turn of the century.

Even the patrons looked different. Familiar. New Yorkers. Types she'd seen all her life. It was only when she left L.A. that she realized how unnatural it was to her. After all these years she'd thought she'd accepted living in a place that sprouted palm trees everywhere. But every so often she found them disconcerting.

"You know, you're a lot more relaxed than I thought you'd be after talking to her," Sarah commented.

"That's probably because I'm too numb to feel it yet," Kate joked.

But even she was surprised. Maybe she was getting better. She'd have to wait until breakfast to find out.

She felt better after talking to Sarah over dinner, and put herself to sleep chanting "A table is a table is a table is a table is. . . ."

They sat across from each other in the restaurant.

Both studied the menu for a long time before Anne finally said, "I never really liked their food."

"I thought you said you wanted to eat here."

"Meet here. That's what I said. I wanted to meet out front and walk to a new place a few blocks away."

"Oops."

"Doesn't matter. I can't say I'm real hungry."

"Me neither," Kate said. Good, at least I'm not the only one who's a nervous wreck.

Kate studied Anne while Anne studied her menu. As much as she wanted to say that Anne didn't look good, Kate couldn't deny what she saw. Although Anne's hair was slightly darker (a result of being out of the sun too long), she didn't have a trace of New York pallor (Kate could always guess which was the flight from New York when she arrived at the airport and saw a gray-green band of passengers straggling towards the baggage claim area). She was wearing pants and a red print shirt Kate hadn't seen before, as well as a new watch. She was not wearing the ring that Kate had had made for her. She was, however, wearing a pair of silver earrings Kate had given her when they had first started going together. They may even have been the first significant present she had given Anne. So long ago that Kate couldn't remember the occasion for the gift. They were a part of Anne she had taken for granted, that's how often she had seen them. They had little meaning anymore.

The waiter came and took their orders and their menus. The last artificial barrier between them was gone.

"You look different," Anne said.

"I'm thinner." Kate was giving her no points for being nice.

"No." Anne held her hand near Kate's face, almost reaching for something, gesturing vaguely. "No, it's around the eyes. A different look."

Kate couldn't say anything. Too many conflicting

feelings going on at once. Overload.

"You look good," Anne concluded.

"Am I supposed to curtsy?" Oh shit, I'm not going to be able to stand myself if I keep this up.

That's how their breakfast had started out. Anne wanting to have a conversation and Kate watching herself push Anne further and further away. Soon there'd be no bringing her back. Then would she be satisfied?

Anne gamely carried on, talking about work, about living in the city again, who was still here that Kate would know, who wasn't. Talking about everything except what was really on each of their minds.

Kate found herself tightening her whole body against anything she might feel for Anne, bracing herself for the pain.

She took the opportunity, when their food came, to take stock, check her wounds.

At first she looked inside just long enough to see if she was in pain. She looked for the hurt and couldn't find it. She looked a little deeper. Still no pain. Only a vague displaced feeling: this was Anne in front of her, reminiscing at that moment about a weekend they had spent in La Jolla. And here was Kate having to remind herself that this was the person she had once thought she'd be with for the rest of her life. And now she wasn't particularly interested in what Anne was saying. Was that possible? That it didn't *matter* to her?

Still, it took her a few minutes to lose the edge she gave herself with Anne. She couldn't let her guard down all at once. She suspected that it would take a while after this to recover completely, some time before she could relax and stop the little pokes she took at Anne. But she realized that those, too, would stop.

For the first time ever with Anne, Kate opened her eyes fully. All she saw sitting across the table from her was a woman about her age, pretty, a little nervous perhaps. Just a person.

Kate didn't say anything to Anne about her new discovery. She needed to explore, play with it a little first, to be sure that it was real.

She started by asking some quetions about Jane.

"So, how are you guys doing?"

Anne paused before answering. "Are you sure you want to know?"

A million sharp answers came to her at once, but Kate wasn't going to be snide. She gritted her teeth and let only one short word squeeze its way out. "Yes."

"Just checking. We're doing fine. Actually, we're very happy."

That was okay. Not too hard to hear. "I'm glad," said Kate. And she guessed she really was. "How's her work going?"

"She's doing really well. She just got another promotion."

There was only so much Kate could think to ask about Jane, only so much she was interested in knowing, and only so much Anne was going to volunteer. That track didn't run very long.

"And how are you two adjusting to living together?" Kate had heard that Anne hadn't wanted to give up her apartment at first.

"We like it a lot."

There, that was too much, that hurt a little. So, thought Kate, not everything is possible. Still, the new freedom, even with its limits, was exhilarating.

Kate relaxed a little. The change was all too new to feel really comfortable yet, but the opening and expanding possibility excited her. She found she could have a conversation with Anne.

Their history was history (a song title if she'd ever come

up with one), time to move forward.

The sensation was like meeting a new person.

They talked for the first time about their relationship, what they'd learned from each other.

"I've grown up a lot, you know," Anne said.

And Kate nodded and agreed, but inside she knew that no matter how much Anne had grown, it wouldn't have been enough. People don't change that much. And she also knew that that was fine.

Kate apologized for being nasty. Anne apologized for leaving her. And Kate felt comfortable enough to say "That's okay, you'll regret it." And there was a tinge of jab to the words, but that was okay, it felt like their first joke, an indication that this was something in the past. Or at least on its way into the past.

When they were on the street saying goodbye, they held each other for a long time. And their embrace really felt like a different kind of goodbye. Kate felt very good holding Anne again. And she was also going to feel fine letting her go.

As Kate walked back uptown, her muscles relaxed and the pressure in her head eased. She wouldn't go so far as to say it was all over, but the end was in sight.

She went to the Museum of Modern Art. As she walked through the rooms, she felt as if she were visiting old friends. She sat in front of "The Starry Night." Not her favorite, she stopped there in honor of hours spent before it in college, when she had been researching a long paper on Van Gogh.

Her mind wandered. She walked into another room. More friends.

Even the Italian Futurists made her smile. Paintings that on first sight had been puzzles requiring hours to solve. But once she'd solved them she could never again see them from the same innocent vantage point.

Her life was falling into place in the same way. Everything that had happened to her recently had turned out to be for the better, somehow. Even having her heart broken had a positive side. Anne had left her and that had forced her to look at what she was doing and what she wanted. She had put too much into Anne, always willing to heap on more when it was clear to her now, in retrospect, that Anne hadn't wanted all that responsibility in the first place.

Nicky was different. Nicky was a lighter side of herself. A hint at a way of being that she could adapt to her own self. She genuinely cared about Nicky but she knew Nicky was right when she had said that they would have to talk when she got back to L.A.

She was leaving something behind. A landscape demarcated on one side by Anne's leaving and on the other by this trip to New York.

Which was all about letting go.

Which she saw as a jumble of events all grouped around the hospital, around Alice. (And with her mother somewhere in the background.) She believed that there were reasons for everything. All of this went together, the breakup, the delay of her movie, Nicky, Alice.

Lauren shimmered in and out of her thoughts. A mixed tapestry of sound and images. Pieces of their conversations woven through her memories of Lauren's eyes, the graceful way she used her hands when she spoke. She thought of Lauren and noticed the way a bright patch of light on a cornerstone wasn't direct sun but a reflection from the glass of a building across the street. Juxtaposition of colors — buildings, billboards, cars. As she wandered around the museum she imagined showing it to Lauren. Every new building or favorite corner, every art deco doorway became something to file away for future reference. The Frick.

The Cloisters. Philip Johnson's house.

She stopped herself abruptly. She didn't even know this woman.

Kate was looking at her favorite Steichen when she remembered she hadn't eaten anything at breakfast. She was very hungry.

She left the museum and stopped at a deli, had a sandwich and a beer, and toasted herself for having figured something out.

She looked at the table. Wood-grained linoleum with a stainless steel edge. There were a few grains of salt around the salt shaker, and a dried spot of ketchup near the wall. But, as for the table itself, it looked pretty much like a table.

Kate usually brought little treats for Alice when she came to visit. Rolls and croissants one day, her favorite cookies (chocolate leaves from a bakery near Kate's apartment) another. Today she decided on something a little more exotic: clementines (little tangerines from Morocco — at least the guy at the fruit stand had *said* they were from Morocco) and kiwi fruit.

Alice got all excited about the kiwi. She thought maybe it was the same fruit she'd first eaten fifty years earlier. She couldn't remember where exactly, though she was pretty sure it had been somewhere in the Far East. . . . Then, with a long sigh, "Ah, Sumatra." (She made it sound like Su-maah-tra.) "But," she continued, "what I ate was pink inside, not green like this. But it tasted like this. Like a mixture of pineapple and strawberry." She asked again what it was called.

"Kiwi," Kate answered.

"Kiahwee?"

"No, Aunt Alice, kiwi. Like 'key' and 'we.' "

After much coaching, she finally got it. "Ah, KIVI! KIVI! That's much easier than ki-AH-wee!"

Kate left it at that.

A nurse came in to check on Alice; she was cheerful, though not overbearingly so. "Well, Dr. Schindler, how are you feeling today?" She moved to the bed and efficiently scooped Alice's wrist between her thumb and fingers and measured her pulse. She continued without missing a beat. "I'll bet you're excited about going home soon."

Actually, neither Alice nor Kate was particularly thrilled at the thought of Alice's going home. Not that Alice enjoyed the hospital. But each knew that Kate would stay a day or so after that, to make sure Alice was settled, then go back to L.A. It was as if Kate's leaving took the place of the final leaving, Alice's dying. Alice had told Kate that she was going to ration the fruit, one half at each meal, so that it would last her the rest of her stay in the hospital. But what she really wanted to do was ration the rest of Kate's time, stretch it to make it last longer.

Kate stayed until visiting hours were over. No one else came to visit Alice that evening, and they both were glad for that.

Kate's last visits with Alice were markedly different from the earlier ones. Yet the differences were subtle. And unspoken. Now everything they said had a subtext. It didn't matter what they talked about, they were really saying goodbye to each other.

Ever since Kate had moved to L.A. Alice had been giving her names of people in the Industry to contact. Alice had been pediatrician to all of them; she referred to them as her babies. Kate usually called the people — not because they could help her — but because she knew they would want to hear about Alice.

Alice was proud of Kate and her successful career. She had always offered Kate thoughts about characters and events, ideas to use in her scripts. Now she was adamant: Kate should write happier stories. "Why concentrate on all that gloomy stuff?"

"I write about things that interest me, Aunt Alice."

"Yes, but always so sad."

Kate should look at life differently. Alice herself had seen so much. She'd had to leave her home in Germany when Hitler came. She'd gone to France, and came from there to the States. Her sister refused to leave Germany; Alice said she spent the war passing as a non-Jew. Alice never saw her again; she refused to have anything to do with her when she finally did come to the States around 1950. Alice's husband was dead; those members of her family who had survived the Holocaust were also dead. She had studied medicine in Germany, been forced to leave, to learn a new language in a new country, to establish herself all over again. She had lost babies, lost parents, lost friends. And through it all her outlook on life was bright, her disposition gentle and forward.

She told Kate a story, "A *true* story," she emphasized, about two people she had studied with in Germany before the war. The couple had been platonic friends who spent all their spare time together. They lost track of each other during the dislocation of the war, married, started families. She ended up in South America, he in New York. They had no idea if the other was still alive. They met, by chance, twenty-five years later at a medical convention, and realized, at age sixty, what they meant to each other, and became lovers. When the convention was over, she went back to her family and her work and he went back to his practice (his wife had died two years earlier). "Why don't you write about that?" Alice concluded.

"But that's not so happy, they didn't end up together,"

Kate said.

"But you wouldn't have to end it that way." It took Alice a little time to bring herself back to the present.

"I'll think about it, I promise."

Just so Kate wouldn't forget, Alice wrote down for her: "University friends." She also added two names to the list, babies she had heard of through proud parents. "They're in L.A., call them. It couldn't hurt."

Kate didn't know if she would call, but she did save the note.

Two days after Alice had gotten out of the hospital, Alice had Kate over to tea. It was their last visit together. "Tea is too much trouble," Kate had protested when she got the invitation.

"I insist. I'm so glad to be back in my house again."

"Well, don't go to a lot of trouble."

"I won't."

But of course Kate knew there would be an assortment of cakes and cookies enough for four.

Going to Alice's had always been like walking into another world. All the things from Germany seemed so out of place. Not out of place in the house, but in the context of Queens, New York. It was like another planet. Like walking off the BMT into the Old World. The furniture was heavy dark wood; high-backed chairs with leather seats loomed around the dining room table, which was a solid mass of dark wood. The armchairs in the living room were big stuffed things that Kate never quite fit into. White lace curtains hung on the windows, as well as beautiful stained glass medallions. The bookcases were filled with leather-bound volumes. Alice wanted to give Kate the complete works of Goethe, "It would be good for your writing," she said. But Kate reminded her that she didn't speak German. "Oh, yah, that was your mother."

Alice's husband Karl had been in the import/export business, and they had lived in Japan. The time they had spent there showed up in the addition to their house. (Maybe this was also the influence of America, and a sign of their wanting to fit in, to have furniture the exact opposite of what they were used to.) The study was a different world. The furniture was low and modern. Teak. Air and light. Buddhas and hangings from the Orient. Evidence of all their travels had found its way to this room, where Alice and Karl were more comfortable than in the stuffy front room, and where they had lived. The coffee table was cluttered with medical journals that Alice still kept up, even though she'd been retired for years. (In fact, Kate had heard her chide one of her doctors for not being up on the latest research.)

The tea Alice prepared for Kate belonged in the German part of the house. There were several different kinds of cakes and cookies, some from a nearby bakery, some from friends, homemade. Alice wouldn't stop serving until Kate had tried at least one of everything.

Kate finally sat back in her chair. "I ate too much. Look." She pulled up her sweater and showed Alice that she had unbuttoned her pants. "I'll have to start exercising the minute I get back to L.A."

"You'll have to swim for me," Alice said. She and Karl used to go to Florida for the winter, and Alice went into the ocean every day. Kate would write jealous letters from New York, asking Alice to take a swim for her.

"It's a deal," Kate said, though they both knew that as often as she went to the beach she rarely went into the water.

When Kate first asked her how she was feeling, Alice had answered fine, but now she admitted, "I don't feel the same. Something's different." She thought the chemotherapy had taken something out of her.

Kate could see that for herself. Alice's good eye, the one

that just a week ago had been clear and strong, was still bright, but dimmed slightly with fear and wonder, as if it said, much more articulately than Alice ever would, Is this really happening?

Alice had been very busy since she'd left the hospital. She was putting everything in order; she didn't want to leave behind confusion as she'd seen so many of her friends do. "Your father's been so good to me. Such a help. He's a good man. And Helen is very nice. Not like your mother, but I think your mother would understand."

She was also going through all her possessions and marking down who should get what. She was going to have her nieces over to pick out what they would like. She had already sorted through her jewelry and paintings. Now came the task of deciding who got the Oriental rugs, the Biedermeier furniture, the big things.

"Laurie should get these linens, because she'll be moving into her own apartment soon, and she'll need them. Karen can have the dishes, she entertains a lot."

Kate trailed Alice through the apartment as she pointed out who got what. The unreality of this, the possibility that someday Alice wouldn't be there, was too much for her to take in. She had to make it into a task, a chore; she was helping her aunt with something that needed to be done, like closing a house for the summer.

When she noticed that Alice was getting tired, she said, "I'm going to leave now. You need to rest. Hannah will be here tomorrow, she can help you with what's left. You take it easy."

"Yes, okay."

They said goodbye and hugged each other, and then Alice unlatched the door and Kate was through it and in the driveway.

As she walked away from the house, Kate turned back and saw Alice looking at her through the venetian blinds.

Just her eyes and her hand were visible. Kate waved to her, then turned and kept walking. She knew Alice was still looking, but she didn't turn back again. She knew that Alice just wanted to watch her. It was Alice saying her last good-bye, making her own memory. Not turning around was Kate's last present to Alice.

Her father called. Kate filled him in on Alice, told him about the kiwi. He said he'd be happy to keep her supplied.

After she got off the phone, Kate sat quietly for a few minutes. Her father had suggested she stay an extra day or two. Kate had declined.

"Are you in any rush to get back?" he'd asked.

"Not really." She paused. "There isn't much else to do here, if you know what I mean."

"Don't worry, you go back. I'll keep an eye on Alice. You were here for the important part."

"Do you think it'll be a lot longer?"

"It's hard to tell."

They didn't talk much after that. Helen got on the phone, said she was very sorry she wasn't going to see Kate, and how was everything going?

After she hung up, Kate turned on the television. She didn't watch it, just needed background noise.

The final goodbye had been so quick. And, in a way, so easy, so normal. This goodbye was so immense that there was no way to deal with its size. They had had to make it sound like every other goodbye they had ever said. Every winter Alice went to Florida, every summer to Connecticut. Kate had gone away on vacations, to camp, to college, to California. They had always said goodbye, and they had always seen each other again. They had acted as if this wasn't going to be any different. They had made it normal.

Their last talks in the hospital had been about everything and nothing in particular. Politics, summers in Connecticut, family ties, new plants for her garden. Alice had so much to tell Kate. Every subject, no matter how inconsequential, was covered with equal intensity. (The conversations reminded Kate of talks she'd had with her mother after her first operation: everything her mother had previously thought boring became something to savor. Driving a car through cross-town traffic was something her mother had thought she'd never be able to do again: getting stuck in rush hour was a luxury because she was alive to be stuck in it.)

And their goodbye was the opposite of those talks. The last goodbye became casual. It had to be. Its very nature dictated that.

It wasn't denial, they weren't fooling each other or themselves. There simply wasn't the mechanism for this, Kate thought, that's not how we're built. There is no way to say goodbye when you know you'll never see each other again.

Kate fell asleep. She woke with a start at ten, not quite sure where she was. She remembered that she had made plans to meet some friends for a drink at one of the women's bars. She called to cancel, then set her alarm because she had to be up early to meet Sarah for breakfast before going to the airport.

Kate called Jennifer in L.A. "I'm sad, Jennifer." They talked for a long time. Stayed away from the big things, Alice and Anne. Stuck to gossip, reports of changes in the city, new restaurants. Kate told Jennifer she was coming back early.

"Is Nicky going to pick you up?"

"I haven't called her."

Jennifer took the flight information. "I'll meet you

outside the baggage claim."

"See you tomorrow."

Kate made herself a cup of tea. She called Nicky, but got the machine. She didn't leave a message.

PART III

Due to strong headwinds, the flight home was very long. The few times Kate dozed off the drone of the engines confused her thoughts. She couldn't remember which direction she was flying, east or west, which was home, New York or Los Angeles. She imagined Nicky waiting for her at the gate, smiled at the thought of her cool hands clearing away the smells and sounds of the hospital. Somewhere underneath that or alongside it Kate realized she must be dreaming because Nicky wasn't going to be at the airport.

Then she was back in a dream inside her dream, walking down the hospital corridor in time to a woman's groans. She walked into Alice's room, and the groaning woman was in a bed near Alice's. Kate was afraid the noise would disturb Alice's sleep. Then there was a racket and clatter outside the door.

Kate woke with a start to see the flight attendants coming down the aisle with the dinner carts.

Kate thought about Nicky while she ate, then dozed again immediately after her meal. The narration in her dream sounded like a textbook, something scientific explaining that what she had had with Nicky had been glandular.

* * * * *

Coming in to LAX was like flying over Shangri-la. The San Bernadino mountains, quiet and green-black, were shrouded in a dreamy mist. Kate knew by now the difference between fog and smog, but from 35,000 feet the noxious haze was benign, if not downright beautiful.

Arriving in L.A. always reminded her of her first impressions of the place, her excitement at the changes she was making in her life. Every so often, even now, she could still recall her New Yorker's amazement at the sight of a row of tall palm trees lining an avenue, or a drive out Sunset Boulevard to the beach (imagine actually *using* Sunset Boulevard to get somewhere!). Her memories were very vivid still, and shot through with bright light.

But not on this flight. Her plane touched down at 2:34 p.m. As soon as it rolled to a stop, Kate immediately forgot all her dreams and decisions. She was wrung out from the trip.

Her suitcase was one of the first off the carousel. Jennifer was waiting outside the terminal and off they went, arriving at Kate's house in twenty minutes.

As unreal as New York had seemed, L.A. appeared even more so now. Kate's mind was still in New York. As she went through her mail, checked on her plants, turned on the sprinklers in the yard, she felt disoriented. A few hours earlier she'd been saying goodbye to Sarah on the corner of 54th and Second. Her tea with Alice could have happened yesterday or last year or possibly not at all. When she unpacked and put away her suitcase, there were no signs that she had been gone. None.

She listened to the messages on her machine. The last was from Nicky. "I know you're not due in for another two days but I really wanted to hear your voice and the machine was better than nothing. And I wanted to welcome you home. Oh — and I can't wait to get you into bed."

* * * * *

Kate showered. As she washed away the stale smell of the airplane, she knew she had made a final decision that she and Nicky shouldn't see each other anymore. It was over, they'd fought off their demons together. Then why not just let it fade out naturally, without going through a whole big thing? But she thought she owed it to Nicky to say something. Not just fade away.

She called Nicky.

"Why didn't you let me know when you were coming?" Nicky asked, disappointed. "I had a surprise planned."

They met at an Italian restaurant on Melrose. The place was empty except for one table of early diners. Kate made a big deal of deciding what to drink because her first moments with Nicky were awkward. Because she didn't know where to begin.

Kate half-listened to details of the surprise Nicky had planned for her — a limo at the airport, chilled champagne and a light dinner at home, then some very hot sex. She was reminded of their first date, when Nicky had rattled on about the music business. Again, she found herself delighted by Nicky's enthusiasm, especially refreshing after the ordeal of her trip.

And face to face with Nicky, Kate couldn't speak any of the thoughts she had so carefully reasoned out. Her relationship with Nicky had never been based on thought. And sitting at the bar with her, their knees touching, Kate again lost track of everything except her desire for Nicky.

Later, lying next to her, Kate smiled at how naive she'd been to think that she could end it over a Campari and soda.

They fell right back into the pattern they had established before Kate left for New York. The pattern that had been imitation to begin with, all the trappings of intimacy without any sense of real love or commitment.

It didn't help matters that part of Kate was still in New York with Alice, imagining what it would be like to go through decades of memories and parcel them out to nieces and nephews and friends. Getting everything ready for a future she wouldn't know anything about.

Kate didn't talk to Nicky about this. Couldn't talk to her about anything that was really important. All she could do was take her to bed, because there they didn't need words.

Soon Kate didn't have time to talk about anything. She got the go-ahead on her movie. Even better, Nancy was negotiating another deal for her. This time to co-produce one of her scripts. This would mean more than just a bigger paycheck for Kate. As writer only, her work on a project would end when production started. As co-producer, she would have a say in choosing the director and in casting. And she would be on the set to do re-writes during shooting.

She called Alice to tell her the good news.

"Then you won't be coming back to New York?" Alice's voice was thin and weak. Whining, as if she were a child who had been deceived: "But you promised you'd be back!"

"Of course I will! The project won't last forever," Kate reassured her.

Alice recovered quickly, re-assuming her adult voice and role. "Of course, I know that. I'm just disappointed."

They went on to another subject, but Alice's tone stayed with Kate long after they had said goodbye. She wondered why they had both pretended they'd see each other again.

Nicky had been spoiled by all the free time, Kate's availability. Long lunches, afternoons in bed. She didn't voice any of her complaints about Kate's return to work, but Kate sensed a difference in her attitude. Or perhaps an indifference.

Kate was having a harder time herself. Her producers took her out to expensive lunches to discuss the final rewrites, which she then went home to complete. She was writing against a deadline. Small things started to annoy her. Nicky was like a little kid, or a big dog, always needing to be entertained. Kate hadn't noticed before. Or maybe she just hadn't cared. Nicky's music invaded the house. "Does that thing have to be on all the time?" Kate snapped at her. Nicky defended herself as she went to turn down the volume: "I asked if it was okay. You said yes."

Kate found it more and more difficult to be with her. She no longer had any patience for Nicky or her music or her friends.

Kate rehearsed what she would tell her. She even went over it with Claire on the phone.

She needn't have bothered.

"Sandy flew down to see me while you were in New York." That was how Nicky began. They were lying in the back yard, Kate reading the New York Times Book Review. Nicky had finished with the L.A. paper and had been quiet for a long time.

"We didn't sleep together," Nicky started to explain.

"That doesn't matter, I mean, I'm just surprised, that's all." Kate wasn't surprised, she was stunned.

"Well, you know, she wanted me to move up there with her. I was the one who didn't want to go." Kate didn't say anything so Nicky continued. "She asked me again."

"What did you tell her?"

"Yes."

For a wild moment Kate thought, I can win her back, she doesn't really want to be with Sandy. But then she caught herself. That was just a reflex action, knee-jerk from when Anne had left her. She genuinely cared for Nicky, and wished her well, and would miss her. She might even be a little hurt that Nicky was the one to initiate the end. But there had never been a question of anything serious. This is just my bruised ego, Kate thought.

Nicky took Kate's long silence as a sign of sadness. "I kept wanting to talk to you. I guess I never really got over her."

The rest of the conversation wasn't important. Neither woman cried. Nor was even particularly sad. As if each was relieved. As if this had less to do with them than with something that had already been ordained.

"This feels real strange." Tentatively, Nicky reached for Kate. "I suppose we should say goodbye."

As they embraced, Kate whispered, "I'm going to miss our lovemaking."

"Me too," confessed Nicky.

They kissed, suddenly awkward with each other, as if maybe this wasn't supposed to happen. Hesitant at first, but not for long.

They made love right there in the grass. With the sun and the birds and music from someone else's stereo floating around them. And that time it really was the last time.

And then Nicky was gone.

Tabula rasa, a clean slate. And no pain. A strange predicament, and hard for Kate to trust its reality; she was alone, but she felt balanced and content. Nicky was gone and by now Anne was an outline, a stranger, someone she didn't quite remember.

In the clarity of hindsight, Kate's heartache about Anne had eased into a vague sadness. A sigh, more like it, of how much in love Kate had been, of what she had wanted that to be. Which had had little bearing on what it actually was.

Kate had no time to consciously think about all this.

Her "vacation" was long gone, she was smack in the middle of overwork.

Gradually she started behaving like a single woman. She went out on occasional dates, let her friends fix her up with people. But she was just testing the waters. And for the most part she was too caught up in her work to be able to concentrate on anything else. As soon as she had finished one set of re-writes, she had started on the next. She was back on schedule, exhausted by the end of a day. She spent most of her evenings alone at home, or at a movie with Eve and Jennifer. That was all she needed.

Once, Jennifer casually introduced Lauren's name into a conversation, then asked, equally casually, if Kate had called her.

"No, Jennifer. And I don't want to talk about it, either."

Jennifer had backed off immediately.

But Kate had thought about Lauren. And had continued to tell herself that she was better off this way, unencumbered, without responsibility.

Actually, Kate had seen Lauren once. They ran into each other at a movie. Kate had forgotten — not exactly forgotten, hadn't remembered correctly, not with the proper intensity — the surprising effect of Lauren's light eyes in contrast to her dark hair. Kate's memory had been one-dimensional, while Lauren in person was anything but. Lauren was with friends, and invited Kate to meet them at a bar later. Kate made excuses.

And was left with a picture of Lauren, just a hint of something she hadn't felt in a long time. Something that could make her happy.

But she didn't know if she trusted her own judgement.

That's what had been so good about being with Nicky.

She had never been in any danger of falling in love or losing herself. She had probably chosen her for just that reason.

There was no chance that she could ever be as blind as she had been about Anne. She couldn't be hurt that way more than once. Not because she wouldn't take any risks again, but because she would be on the lookout for signs. And as well as Kate knew all this, she wasn't ready to test the depth of her new knowledge. She wasn't ready to jump into anything.

And she could see jumping into Lauren.

Something about this woman frightened her, something Kate couldn't quite identify. Yet she felt foolish making such a big deal about someone she didn't know. They had spent only a few hours together; they hadn't even been alone during that time. Probably all she was doing was putting Lauren's face on True Love's imaginary perfect woman. Probably.

Seeing each other again was inevitable, and it happened at a brunch at someone's place out at the beach. Even as she parked the car Kate sensed Lauren's presence. She told herself she was being ridiculous. She didn't even know if her hostess knew Lauren.

She was greeted enthusiastically by several women. She saw Emily in a corner with some young thing, and was on her way over there when someone tapped her on the shoulder. Kate turned and was face to face with Lauren.

"Hello."

Kate felt cornered. She made small talk and wondered where her friends were when she needed them. On cue, Emily waved to her. "Excuse me, I've got to say hello to someone."

Not that Emily helped any. After introducing her to her friend ("Susie's from New York. You should have a lot in common." Yeah, if I were fifteen years younger, thought Kate), Emily started in on Kate about Lauren. "I need a drink," said Kate. "Nice meeting you," she said to Susie, and walked away.

She stepped outside onto the balcony and slid shut the glass door. She had butterflies in her stomach. She took a few deep breaths to calm herself. She leaned on the railing and watched the weekend beach activity below.

The door slid open and shut. Lauren leaned on the railing next to her.

Lauren waited a moment before speaking. "This may sound very strange, since I hardly even know you. But I think you've been avoiding me."

"I don't know you well enough to avoid you."

"That's what I thought. But have you?"

Kate dropped back and punted. "Want to go for a walk?"

"Do you always answer a question with a question?"

"A lot of my friends are therapists."

They walked down to the beach. A few miles up the coast, the Santa Monica Pier balanced out over the water. Once they were together, Kate couldn't for the life of her remember what it was she'd been fighting. Walking along the sand with this black-haired, gray-eyed, beautiful woman seemed the least frightening thing she'd done in a long time.

At one point she even admitted to Lauren that she had in fact avoided her.

"Why were you afraid of me?" Lauren wondered.

"I don't know. I heard about Chris . . ."

"And you thought I'd be grabbing on to the first woman I met. I know I can't replace her, I'm not trying to. It's taken me over two years to feel normal again. Problem is, now that I'm 'back,' everyone wants to fix me up with someone."

"I know what that's like."

"I did it a few times, more for my friends than for myself. I'm happy enough with my work. For now."

That was a beginning. After their walk, there was no way not to go forward.

But slowly. For the first time in her life, Kate was determined to keep her breath. All those weeks of thinking about Lauren, of not letting herself think about Lauren. She could never be what I've built her up to be, Kate thought.

But the more time they spent together, the more the reality of this woman reached the level of fantasy.

The fact that they were both very busy affected the pace of their beginning. But being forced to go slowly heightened the excitement.

When Kate wasn't actually with Lauren, she was thinking about her. She sat at her desk and instead of working on her revisions wrote what she knew about Lauren: She was close to her parents in Northern California, had spent a great deal of time with them after Chris died. She had spent fifteen years building her business, and had taken refuge in it for the last two. Now she knew what she wanted. Chris' sudden death had put things into perspective for her, made her re-evaluate her priorities.

Kate then tried to describe how beautiful Lauren was, with dark hair and light eyes; high coloring.

Frustrated, she tore the page out of the typewriter. She wasn't a descriptive writer, and couldn't do justice to this woman. She went back to what she was good at, dialogue, her mind wandering off every so often to dream of Lauren.

One Friday evening Kate arrived at Lauren's office to pick her up for dinner. Lauren was still in a meeting; she popped her head out to say she'd be ready soon.

While she waited, Kate studied the pictures all over the walls of the reception area. Photographs of completed jobs, magazine layouts of houses and buildings Lauren had designed, framed awards and citations. She moved into Lauren's area, sat at her desk, which was a drafting table.

Lauren's office was not a separate room with a door. She was accessible to questions from her staff and yet could work without having to answer a phone every five minutes. There were templates and triangles and eraser shields hanging next to her work table, and when Lauren worked she faced a bulletin board cluttered with specifications, order forms, notes to herself, a picture of herself with her family.

Kate heard the meeting breaking up, people leaving. She felt Lauren's presence before she saw her.

"Sorry that took so long."

"No problem. I made myself comfortable." And when Kate turned to Lauren, something about the way she was standing and the light in the office, which was coming only from the windows and the skylight (and there was a particularly spectacular Los Angeles evening sky), something about all of it plus Lauren's natural beauty combined to make the reality of Lauren eclipse the fantasy.

Kate wanted to tell Lauren she looked beautiful but no words came to her. There was more than physical beauty. The room changed for Kate when Lauren walked in. Kate opened her mouth, closed it again. No way to tell Lauren what she felt at that moment. And yet somehow she knew that there was no need to tell her. She wanted to go to Lauren and didn't know what was holding her back. Neither of them moved. They stood across the room from each other but they could have been touching.

Someone had to break the spell.

"I like this," Kate said. "This" was a model of a house on the table. Kate crossed the room to stand near the table.

"It's a massing model. I wanted to study the scale of the

building in relationship to its surroundings. Also ideas for some of the details of the building itself. Like here." She moved to the model and showed Kate where some cardboard had been added to one wall. "I wanted to see what would happen if I took a big chunk of wall away and put in glass instead. I didn't like it."

"Is this the Santa Barbara house?"

The house was one of the reasons she had seen so little of Lauren in the last two weeks. Lauren had had to drive up to check on its progress.

After Kate looked at the model, Lauren showed her the blueprints and plans. "It's like a foreign language," said Kate. In addition to being able to read the blueprints, Lauren knew how to talk to contractors and plumbers and roofers. She knew about building codes and restrictions, hardscape and roof plans, the HVAC package (which Kate now knew meant heat, ventilation, and air conditioning).

Lauren showed her flimsies of the house, conceptual drawings on what looked like brown tracing paper that came on a roll. Kate saw electrical plans, reflected ceiling plans, topographical, foundation, and framing plans. She looked at the engineering sheet, cross-sectional studies, and exterior and interior elevations of the house.

And all during this time, Lauren's arm brushed against Kate's as she reached for a piece of paper, their fingers touched as they passed drawings back and forth. Their thighs touched as they sat together looking at ideas for the new project. No matter how hard Kate tried to concentrate on the papers in front of her, the sexual energy between her and Lauren was so great that it sent chills through her.

That they were moving towards a relationship was a given. Inevitable, just as their meeting at the party had been.

Three weeks of lunches and dinners and museums and galleries had given Kate a chance to pace herself. Yet the fear she had experienced when Lauren stood next to her on the balcony at the beach hadn't completely dissolved. There was still a barrier to be dropped.

The question of their future hung between them.

Kate drove Lauren back to the office after dinner so that she could pick up her car. Before she got out of the Alfa, Lauren asked, "Want to come with me to the Santa Barbara house tomorrow?"

"I thought you'd never ask. I'm dying to see this place in the flesh, or whatever the correct architectural term is."

"We've got to get up very early," Lauren said.

"That's okay," Kate said. Although she suspected that she was supposed to be taking a hint: Lauren would pick her up at seven the next morning, but why make her go through all the trouble? Why not spend the night together?

Kate surprised herself. Under normal circumstances, she would have leapt long ago. Probably on the first date. And now, even with this perfect opening, she didn't move any closer to Lauren. But she could tell they were on the edge of the barrier.

Their goodnight kiss was a kind of contract, a way of ending the evening and of promising more.

They took the coastal route up to Santa Barbara. A little longer, but much prettier. The water was dark gray, not blue-green yet because of some late-night-early-morning-low-clouds. "That's one of my favorite California expressions," said Kate. "We don't have that in New York. It's either sunny or cloudy or rainy or whatever. We never have anything as good as late-night-early-morning-low-clouds."

There were no clouds by the time they got to Santa

Barbara. As they started winding into the hills, Lauren pointed up to some extensive framework. "That's us."

Lauren turned onto a narrow private road a few miles past the entrance to a reservoir. As the Saab bounced up the rutted path, Lauren explained that the road wouldn't be paved until the house was finished. "In the meantime, I've considered buying a jeep just for this project."

They parked under some trees and walked towards the house. Or the skeleton of the house. Lauren indicated where the garage would be, how the driveway would curve to the front door, how the front of the house would be landscaped.

They paused at the main entrance. And even though Kate couldn't read construction language, the details or fine print, she could see that there was a view from the front door down what was going to be a long hallway to the living room and right out the living room window. Visitors would be still catching their breath from the beautiful drive up to the house only to have it knocked out of them again by the spectacular view of the pool over the reservoir over the ocean.

Lauren walked Kate through the house, Kate remembering the flimsies and drawings she had seen the night before. Still she had a hard time translating the framing into what she had understood of the blueprints. More than ever, this was a foreign language. There were letters she could read, words she could recognize, but the whole thing remained basically unintelligible. She wasn't sure how much of it would have made sense had she not seen the massing model.

Lauren finished with the contractor sooner than she had expected. She suggested a walk in town before lunch.

A little over an hour's drive from Los Angeles, Santa Barbara stretched tastefully up from the ocean into the Santa Ynez mountains. A quiet, relaxed beach town. With, Kate noticed as they walked around, branches of most of the major brokerage houses scattered throughout the town's little shops and restaurants. Merrill Lynch, Dean Witter Reynolds, E. F. Hutton. A lot of old money in Santa Barbara.

Kate and Lauren wandered in and out of stores, enjoying each other's company more than the browsing. They passed a Mexican restaurant in an open courtyard and realized they were hungry. Kate left the decision of where to eat up to Lauren. "This is your territory."

"There's a restaurant up in the hills with a wonderful view."

What Lauren hadn't said about the restaurant was that it was connected to a hotel.

Tour books would have described it as charming. The grounds were tree-shaded and impeccably landscaped, with cottages that had a wonderful air — not quite run-down, more shabby-genteel. The main building of the hotel offered a spectacular view of the town and harbor.

When Kate and Lauren were seated at their patio table, with Santa Barbara looking very European below them, Lauren excused herself to wash up.

While she was gone, Kate spoke to the concierge. When Lauren came back to the table, Kate said "I took the liberty of getting us a room."

Lauren smiled. "I thought you'd never ask."

Kate knew exactly how she was going to make love to Lauren. She had already imagined it.

They would undress and lie on the bed. They would do everything slowly. That would be the key: everything slow and deep.

She would look at Lauren. She wouldn't touch her right away. Or maybe just ever so softly, to trace the sides of her body, barely touching, moving slowly down from her face to her neck to her hip and thigh, the hollow behind her knee. Lauren would be lying on her back. And Kate would hover over her, legs between Lauren's legs, supporting herself on her arms, and then lower herself onto Lauren. Slowly. Lower herself into a kiss and the softness of her lover's body.

Of course that wasn't how it happened at all.

Kate, in her imagining of the moment, had forgotten to take into account how beautiful Lauren would be. That Lauren's skin would be cool and smooth and tanned. That there might be birds singing outside.

Her original plans, she realized, had been nothing more than a road map.

None of it was awkward, nothing got in the way. The first time they made love was fast, not too fast, but not the kind of exploring Kate had expected. It was only after that that they took their time to learn about each other.

Kate kissed the hollow where Lauren's neck met her shoulder. "I've been wanting to do that for weeks."

They talked about how they'd felt during the time they'd spent together, how hard it had been to stay away from each other, maintain equilibrium.

"I've wanted this ever since that night Eve and Jennifer introduced us," Lauren confessed, trailing her fingers up and down Kate's side.

The admission excited and frightened Kate. She was still keeping a partial barrier between them.

Lauren must have sensed this, because she said "Don't worry, I'm a very patient person." She added an afterthought. "I never used to be that way. Chris was always trying to slow me down."

And then Lauren told Kate about Chris. Not for the first time, but for the first time in this way — offering Kate her history.

Kate reciprocated by talking about Anne. As she talked she felt a strangeness, as if it had all happened to someone else. And in a way it had. Kate wasn't the same anymore.

She understood more and more clearly where she had gone wrong, how she had done as much to push Anne away as Anne had done to distance herself. Kate was still unwilling to make the same mistake. So hard for her to see Lauren as someone different, not Anne.

Kate didn't tell Lauren that last part.

But, "I'm not Anne, you know," Lauren said when Kate had finished. "And you're not Chris."

"Basically I know that." Too much of this talk scared Kate.

Lauren, seeking to reassure her, took Kate's hand and moved it between her legs, eased Kate's fingers inside. She held Kate's hand tight against her. Kate could feel Lauren open inside, so that there was space around her fingers. Then Lauren contracted her muscles and tightened around Kate.

With her leg Kate spread Lauren's legs further apart, then she wrapped her legs around Lauren's thigh. She brought Lauren's other hand to her mouth. She kissed Lauren's palm, tongued between her fingers. Kate was ready to come, and Lauren hadn't touched her yet. She pushed herself agaisnt Lauren's legs, her fingers moving faster and faster inside Lauren.

They were lost now, close to coming, neither attached in any way to this earth. Lauren cried "Take me" as she came, and Kate buried deeper into her, holding on for life.

Never before had Kate taken such pleasure in her partner's pleasure. They fell asleep and woke and made love again. They talked. They called room service, showered, ate, went back to bed.

"There should be a special language for this," Kate said. She looked at her hand stroking Lauren's thigh. She wanted a word that had no meaning other than the softness of a breast, another that would mean the smooth skin on the inner thigh. Too many things can be soft or smooth or like silk. "Maybe this is what it feels like to think in pictures."

Lauren pulled Kate to her, kissed her. Then Kate lay beside Lauren, hand over her heart. "My nerves," she said. "Surely we're too old for this."

Lauren was perfectly calm. Serious. "My name isn't Shirley."

It hadn't been that funny. Corny, both knew, but it was all in the delivery. Kate hadn't laughed that hard in ages. Neither of them had. Whooping and hooting and crying. Lying side by side on a bed in a room in a hotel on a hill overlooking Santa Barbara. It was like knowing nothing would go wrong, ever again.

They had breakfast in their room. They had wanted to check out early and go down to the beach, but new beginnings can't be scheduled. Too many opportunities for exploration presented themselves: too many nooks and crannies on a new lover, too many ways to make love.

They left the hotel right at check-out time, noon.

On the drive back, both were very quiet. They again took the coastal route. Kate knew it was just her mood that made the water bluer and clearer than it had been the day before.

Everything that day stood out, was somehow out of the ordinary. Everything would become a memory, everything would become "Remember when we drove down from Santa Barbara...." Part of their history, a magic time to invoke when the initial magic had worn off.

Kate watched Lauren at the wheel. Looked at her strong hands, the hollow of her throat. She had a different relationship to these now. Without thinking about it, Kate reached over and gently stroked Lauren's cheek with the back of her hand. Lauren turned to her, delighted, surprised. "What was that for?"

Kate just shrugged. "Nothing in particular. Because it was there."

Later, Kate would tell her how significant everything had been in the weeks that had led to Santa Barbara, how that time had been so new, everything so clear and sharp in her thoughts. How those weeks had a whole different atmosphere from the days and months surrounding them.

She began a silent dialogue. It's like all beginnings, she told herself, this is how they've all been.

And then she had to point out: but this one is different.

But that's how they'd all been.

Still, this one.

Back and forth, always left with the same idea: All things were possible. Just like the last time. Only this wasn't the last time.

Kate turned from Lauren to the road and for a time the road was a screen on which she saw relationships of her past. They had all begun with a similar golden time. A general feeling of suspension from everyday life, or of soaring above it in the new passion. Whatever happened during that time happened inside the cloud of those all-encompassing feelings. And after the relationship was over, that time remained, separate from what had followed. It was sensory, more a general feeling than specific memories.

And now with Lauren it was happening again. The beginning of the beginning. Everything that they did would take on a glow, a meaning separate from everything else. A time to organize their lives around this new center.

Kate looked out the window. She saw movement on the water, far from shore. At first she wasn't sure what it was, reflections on the waves, maybe a kelp bed. But then it was unmistakable. Dolphins. She had never seen so many before. She pointed them out to Lauren, who pulled over to the side of the road. They got out and watched for a while.

They leaned against the side of the car, almost touching, not talking. Maybe they were watching the dolphins. Maybe they were taking a moment to slow down. The dolphins jumped and were suspended over the water. And as long as Kate and Lauren continued to watch, they themselves would be suspended where they were, halfway between Santa Barbara and L.A. It was a way to hold the moment, postpone re-entry, to catch their breath.

As they paused there to let the significance of the moment sink in, there was never any question that their lives had changed, or that L.A. would be a different city when they returned.

Cynics called it "teenage heaven." That time when nothing else matters because you don't notice that there is anything else. Friends, introductions, dinners and parties would come later. But for now, just each other. There was business to attend to. Buying presents and sending cards and writing love letters and getting together every chance they could.

They called each other several times a day. Sometimes they had something specific to say, sometimes they just wanted to hear each other's voice.

They spent Sundays in bed. (Lauren worked on Saturdays, and took Sunday and Monday off. Kate couldn't take Mondays during pre-production, but looked forward to being back on a flexible writer's schedule.) They talked and read and made love and watched television. They made picnics for the beach but often got no further than Lauren's pool.

It was very quiet at Lauren's. She lived up in the hills and her house was surrounded by trees. Very private. She and Kate swam and lay in the sun and made love in the jacuzzi.

Word was out by now that they were official, and they were swamped with invitations. "We haven't seen you in such a long time," "We can't wait to meet her, we're so glad to hear you're happy," "What are you doing Saturday night?" They could have been busy every night of the week.

Kate had never looked better. That's what everyone told her. Even her agent noticed. (Although Nancy attributed part of Kate's glow to the fact that she was now back at work.)

Friends were starting to ask when she and Lauren were going to move in together. At first, Kate could joke away the questions. But Lauren was only willing to joke so much about Kate's reluctance to make a commitment.

What a relief to throw herself into pre-production flurries, all the last-minute details. Meetings and re-writes and casting sessions. And then, once production started, long hours on the set. She had a new family, the cast and crew of her movie.

She kept putting off even a discussion of their moving in together. "Once we're out of pre-production" became "As soon as the shoot is over I'll be able to think about it."

Kate was afraid of losing Lauren, but at this point was still more afraid of losing herself.

Since New York, Kate had continued to call her aunt every week. Then, after trying unsuccessfully for several days to reach her, Kate called her father and found out that Alice was back in the hospital.

He called Kate a few days later. "They think probably tonight," he said.

"Can I talk to her?" Kate sensed that there was no point in asking even before her father answered that Alice was past that now.

Lauren held Kate that evening and let her talk. "Did I already tell you this?" Kate would ask.

"Tell me again," Lauren would say.

And Kate would tell for the first time, or maybe the third, some story about Alice.

"When I got my first answering machine, when I was still in New York, she thought that when I said 'Leave me a message after the beep' that I was saying I'd gone to the beach. So I'd come home and listen to my messages and there she'd be, wondering why I was going to the beach in November. I explained it to her once. 'The *beep*, Aunt Alice, after you hear the *beep*.' 'Not the beach?' 'BEEP.' 'Ah, that makes much more sense.' But she did it again after that. 'Kate, darling, I hope you're having a good time at the beach. This is your Aunt Alice. Please call me.' "

She told Lauren about Alice's medical practice, about her "children," what she knew about Alice's experiences during the war. Talked about how she wanted to write about Alice and her friends, those women who had come from Germany and settled in a new country and resumed their lives, some of them even starting new careers.

A lot of the stories were about Kate's mother also, stories about Alice that Kate had heard when she was growing up.

"I wish I could be with her tonight."

"I think she probably knows you're there." Lauren stroked Kate's hair, kissed the top of her head.

Kate tried to stay up all night, to keep Alice company during her vigil, but she eventually fell asleep.

She didn't sleep well. Kept opening her eyes and looking at the clock. Not quite awake: 12:50, she's still alive, Kate said to herself. Then she went back to sleep. 2:14, she's still alive. Kate rolled over. 3:30, she's alive. Then there was a time, about an hour after that, that Kate said, almost casually, as if part of a dream, "Oh, she's dead now," and went back to sleep. Though not for ong. She woke around five, very sad, and with a headache.

She called her father a few hours later.

"Around 7:30 this morning," was all he said. "That would have been 4:30 your time."

Kate cried a little, but mostly was quiet. She had prepared herself for this, yet was still in shock. Lauren held her, and was gentle and loving.

Kate dried her eyes and said, "I've got to get to the set."

"Are you sure you want to go today?"

"It's not a hard day. I'd rather keep busy."

But it was a hard day. Not because she had too much to do. That would have been easier. The day's shoot was dull. The location was a small supermarket. The scene simply the main character telling a friend about another friend who was having an affair. And it took all day for that to happen. And Kate watched take after take, the choreography of people and carts. She watched extras picking up the same head of lettuce, the same bunch of grapes. Real shoppers, gathered at one end of the produce section out of camera range, were allowed to scoot to the bins in between takes to get what they needed. Sometimes one of the crew would help select something, more to get them out of the way than to be nice.

Kate called Lauren during the lunch break.

"How's it going?"

"Okay."

"You sound beat."

"It's all kind of unreal."

"I'll take you out to dinner tonight, we can toast Alice."

"Maybe."

"Or whatever. We'll see how you feel."

Kate went to the catering wagon and ordered a salad,

then gave most of it to the sound man because she wasn't
hungry. She sat with some of the cast, listened to them
talk about what else was shooting around town, who was out
of town on location, what projects everyone had lined up
next. But she was miles away, with Alice.

The day of the funeral, Kate awoke in a dark mood. She
planned to spend the day at the beach. She was going to
bring a pad and pen and a book, but mostly the day was for
saying goodbye to Alice. She had no idea how long she'd
stay.

She had decided not to go back for the service. It wasn't
as if Alice were going to be there.

Lauren made her breakfast. A beautiful omelette with
goat cheese and tomatoes and fresh basil. They ate outside
by the pool because it was a glorious day, even if Kate was
wrapped in her dark cloud.

Lauren asked, "What time do you think you'll be back
from the beach?"

Kate was non-commital. Lauren had been wonderful,
and wanted to be close. And every gesture, every word,
even making the omelette, bothered Kate. She wanted to
shrug Lauren off.

Lauren was going up to Santa Barbara to check on the
house. "Sure you don't want to come?" Lauren reached
for Kate's hand. "Maybe they have our room at the hotel."

Kate let Lauren take her hand, but made no other
physical response to the gesture, none of the usual return
squeezes. "What I'm doing today is very important to me."

"I know that." Lauren withdrew her hand. "I thought
maybe you'd like to go to the beach up there and then I'd
come and get you when I was done."

"I am not a child. I can go to the beach by myself."

Kate saw what she was doing but couldn't stop herself.

She had taken the position that Lauren wasn't taking her grief seriously (patently a false position, she could admit to herself). She was pushing Lauren away when she needed her most.

Lauren knew that. "Don't do this, Kate."

"Just leave me alone."

"I don't think you want to be alone."

"Yes I do!"

And Kate pushed until Lauren was angry. Which was what she'd been waiting for, because now Lauren would leave and then Kate could feel sorry for herself because Lauren was walking out. And she could accuse Lauren of not being there. "See, I can't trust you to be there."

Lauren turned to her. "No. You can't trust yourself." When she was excited, aroused, embarrassed, and, Kate now learned, angry, her coloring rose. She was so incredibly beautiful that Kate had a hard time listening to what Lauren was saying. "You say you can't trust me because every time you trusted someone they left. Bullshit. I know about being left. I'm sorry about your aunt, but don't throw her at me as an excuse. I'm sick of waiting for you to make up your mind. I want to be with you. Not just until the heat goes. Maybe it won't last forever, but I need to know that we're working towards something. I want a home. I want left-overs, for chrissake."

Kate didn't say anything. She couldn't deal with Lauren. This was her day for Alice.

"I'll ask you again. Want to come with me?"

Kate had turned away from Lauren. She didn't turn back to answer the question, merely shook her head and offered a muffled "No."

"Fine. It's getting late. I've got to go."

Kate didn't hear Lauren go inside, but then the screen door slammed. She turned to the house. Almost followed.

But she was too stubborn. And what would she have said?

Kate spread out her blanket and sat in her beach chair. The beach wasn't as hot as she had expected it to be. There were a lot of clouds, unusual for July in California. She could hear Claire: "The climate's changing. That's what you get for sending men to the moon." Kate wanted to tell Lauren about that, about Claire and her theories. But Lauren was in Santa Barbara. And they were fighting.

It was still early. In New York, the funeral wouldn't start for a few hours. Kate began her own ceremony. She began to list all that she would miss about Alice. Thoughts about her segued naturally into thoughts about her mother.

And for some reason Anne kept intruding. Starting with odd little things — nicknames they'd given each other, certain mannerisms Anne had — and then whole scenes from their time together. Kate couldn't understand it at first. But then she began to see Anne's place with the other two. The women who had left her.

Kate realized now that Anne's leaving had triggered something for her. Her mother. The loss of Anne had been that loss all over again.

And I walked right into it, Kate thought. Always safe in asking for more because I knew I wasn't going to get it. In some part of her mind, she had known that they weren't going to last.

And by being with someone who left, she could be right about relationships: you got together, you got close, and then the other person vanished. It was really very simple.

And Anne hadn't been the first. She had always chosen women who would prove her theory. Before Anne there had been a few "straight" women, a few free spirits. And afterward, no one who posed a threat of permanency.

Until Lauren.

And this time, Kate was in a different position.

This time, Kate had gone through with her mourning for both Anne and Alice, not cut it off like she had with her mother.

She remembered when she was in college, and a friend had persuaded her to see the college psychologist, a friendly woman in her mid-fifties. A nice mother figure, thought Kate, trying to second-guess her feelings when she first met her.

"Why are you here?" the woman had asked.

"My mother died six months ago and I'm still upset," Kate had answered matter-of-factly.

And then the psychologist explained that six months was not a long time. Was, in fact, not very much time at all to get over something like the death of a parent. And, a horrifying thought to Kate at the time — these feelings would last a long time, "In fact, they might always be there in some form."

But still Kate had hidden from them. First in her school work, then in her career.

And now, sixteen years later, Kate was finally able to integrate them into her life.

Alice came back to her then. Kate was beginning to see Alice's part in this.

She had been able to do things for Alice she hadn't been able to do for her mother. Just sitting there with her, with all those unanswerable questions floating around them in the hospital room — it didn't matter that there had been so much silence. Even something as simple as bringing Alice a bag of kiwi and clementines had made a difference.

Kate jumped from Anne, back to Alice, to her mother again. She had been holding onto the pain so that she could remember these women, afraid that without the pain there would be no memories at all. But her experiences with Anne and Alice, which she had followed to their end and beyond, had taught her differently. Had given her the chance to do it right, enabled her to finally let go.

And suddenly: no more ghosts. Not of her mother, not of Anne. Time, by itself, hadn't been enough to teach her that. Being able to say goodbye to Alice, really *do* it, be there as much as she could, was what enabled her to go on now without carrying these three women along with her. Memories, yes, but not burdens.

Ideas whizzed by so fast that she couldn't name them all. Her thoughts gathered and moved and changed shape like the clouds she was watching.

And Lauren was the sun behind them.

That stopped her in her tracks. She was glad she hadn't written that down, would have been embarrassed by the metaphor. But it was so clear to her. She'd been so afraid of Lauren because she knew that Lauren wasn't going to run away. She knew that Lauren was different from Anne, but that's not what had scared her. Lauren had been right: Kate didn't trust herself. Her fear had nothing to do with Anne or Chris. Lauren was not Anne. But what if Kate was still the same Kate, what if she hadn't learned anything from all this?

She wanted to rush back to Lauren, explain what had happened, why she'd fought with her. Apologize. Tell her all the revelations. She even thought of driving up to Santa Barbara.

But what if Lauren had her own epiphany? Kate would have to wait to find out if she'd completely ruined things.

So she stayed at the beach. She needed to have a talk with Alice. And with her mother.

She didn't leave until she had said goodbye to each of them.

When she got home, she left a message on Lauren's

machine. She apologized. At great length. She asked Lauren to come over: "I know you've driven for hours already, but I could make it worth your while."

She regretted that last bit, that stupid attempt at humor. Lauren didn't have any idea of Kate's new outlook. At best she's probably still mad at me, Kate thought.

After showering, Kate took out chicken and vegetables and started to make something for dinner. Just in case. Part of her believed that Lauren wouldn't even call.

And the whole time she was showering and dressing and cooking — in fact, ever since she'd left the beach, she thought of Lauren. Of living with her. She even went into details: her house or mine? Or would we get a place together? Emily knew a good mover. But then Lauren must know a dozen.

Kate tried to slow herself down but once she'd started on this line there was no stopping. How could Lauren not come back to her? Kate was head-over-heels in love and balanced at the same time. She was a nervous wreck.

Later, she admitted that she didn't know how she'd been able to prepare dinner, she had been so nervous. Putting things away in the wrong place, standing in front of the open refrigerator and not remembering what it was she wanted.

Kate felt the same butterflies in her stomach as when Lauren had walked out to her on the balcony that afternoon at the beach. Today she had ascended to a great height and hadn't yet come down. And this was only the beginning.

Kate wanted a word for what they would have. The only one that came to mind was marriage. And not in the casual sense that a lot of gay women used to describe their relationships, affairs that ended with the passion. Kate wanted the old-fashioned, till-death-do-us-part kind, with growth and movement and maybe occasional boredom.

Kate wanted someone to struggle with, to build a life with. She'd never thought like this before. She caught a glimpse of herself in a mirror and stopped to check her reflection, to touch the glass, make sure she was really there.

Lauren came to Kate directly from Santa Barbara, without checking her machine.

Kate met her at the door and they fell into each other.

Lauren apologized for bringing up a touchy subject at the worst possible time, felt she'd been insensitive. "I've been so worried about you all day, I didn't know what to do."

Kate kissed her quiet. Then took a long time for her own apology. First with words and then with her body.

This is what they'd been moving towards from the first night they'd met, this moment when they said they would be together.

They made love again and this time was different from any other in Kate's life. For the first time this woman was the woman who was going to be there, and there would be no others. This time they both cried as they made love.

As Lauren lay sleeping, Kate walked around her house. She looked in all the rooms. She sat in her office. She imagined setting it up somewhere else. What would she bring with her, what would be left behind.

She went into the kitchen. The dinner she had made was still on the counter, covered up. Kate picked it up to put it in the refrigerator. Lauren stood in the doorway, wearing only a T-shirt. She asked sleepily "What are you doing up?"

"We forgot dinner." Kate smiled at her.

"I know. I'm hungry."

"Now that you mention it, so am I."

They took their plates into the living room and ate. It was two in the morning and they were the only people alive at that moment. They had talked about building a life together and having children but that was the future. This was now. And the present felt like a new planet to Kate.

"Do you think this counts as our first leftovers?" she asked Lauren.

"No. I don't think leftovers are official until you're actually living with someone."

As they ate and talked, Kate still had butterflies in her stomach. The potential for their life together filled the room.

"So." Kate looked at Lauren. When she had read in novels about a character's heart pounding so loudly she couldn't hear, she had never believed it possible. Until now. "Want to get married?"

"I thought you'd never ask."

A few of the publications of
THE NAIAD PRESS, INC.
P.O. Box 10543 • Tallahassee, Florida 32302
Mail orders welcome. Please include 15% postage.

Spring Forward/Fall Back by Sheila Ortiz Taylor. A novel. 288 pp.
ISBN 0-930044-70-3 $7.95

For Keeps by Elisabeth C. Nonas. A novel. 144 pp.
ISBN 0-930044-71-1 $7.95

Torchlight to Valhalla by Gail Wilhelm. A novel. 128 pp.
ISBN 0-930044-68-1 $7.95

Lesbian Nuns: Breaking Silence edited by Rosemary Curb and
Nancy Manahan. Autobiographies. 432 pp.
ISBN 0-930044-62-2 $9.95
ISBN 0-930044-63-0 $16.95

The Swashbuckler by Lee Lynch. A novel. 288 pp.
ISBN 0-930044-66-5 $7.95

Misfortune's Friend by Sarah Aldridge. A novel. 320 pp.
ISBN 0-930044-67-3 $7.95

A Studio of One's Own by Ann Stokes. Edited by Dolores
Klaich. Autobiography. 128 pp. ISBN 0-930044-64-9 $7.95

Sex Variant Women in Literature by Jeannette Howard Foster.
Literary history. 448 pp. ISBN 0-930044-65-7 $8.95

A Hot-Eyed Moderate by Jane Rule. Essays. 252 pp.
ISBN 0-930044-57-6 $7.95
ISBN 0-930044-59-2 $13.95

Inland Passage and Other Stories by Jane Rule. 288 pp.
ISBN 0-930044-56-8 $7.95
ISBN 0-930044-58-4 $13.95

We Too Are Drifting by Gale Wilhelm. A novel. 128 pp.
ISBN 0-930044-61-4 $6.95

Amateur City by Katherine V. Forrest. A mystery novel. 224 pp.
ISBN 0-930044-55-X $7.95

The Sophie Horowitz Story by Sarah Schulman. A novel. 176 pp.
ISBN 0-930044-54-1 $7.95

The Young in One Another's Arms by Jane Rule. A novel.
224 pp. ISBN 0-930044-53-3 $7.95

The Burnton Widows by Vicki P. McConnell. A mystery novel.
272 pp. ISBN 0-930044-52-5 $7.95

Old Dyke Tales by Lee Lynch. Short stories. 224 pp.
ISBN 0-930044-51-7 $7.95

Daughters of a Coral Dawn by Katherine V. Forrest. Science
fiction. 240 pp. ISBN 0-930044-50-9 $7.95

The Price of Salt by Claire Morgan. A novel. 288 pp.
ISBN 0-930044-49-5 $7.95

Against the Season by Jane Rule. A novel. 224 pp.
ISBN 0-930044-48-7 $7.95

Lovers in the Present Afternoon by Kathleen Fleming. A novel.
288 pp. ISBN 0-930044-46-0 $8.50

Toothpick House by Lee Lynch. A novel. 264 pp.
ISBN 0-930044-45-2 $7.95

Madame Aurora by Sarah Aldridge. A novel. 256 pp.
ISBN 0-930044-44-4 $7.95

Curious Wine by Katherine V. Forrest. A novel. 176 pp.
ISBN 0-930044-43-6 $7.50

Black Lesbian in White America by Anita Cornwell. Short stories,
essays, autobiography. 144 pp. ISBN 0-930044-41-X $7.50

Contract with the World by Jane Rule. A novel. 340 pp.
ISBN 0-930044-28-2 $7.95

Yantras of Womanlove by Tee A. Corinne. Photographs.
64 pp. ISBN 0-930044-30-4 $6.95

Mrs. Porter's Letter by Vicki P. McConnell. A mystery novel.
224 pp. ISBN 0-930044-29-0 $6.95

To the Cleveland Station by Carol Anne Douglas. A novel.
192 pp. ISBN 0-930044-27-4 $6.95

The Nesting Place by Sarah Aldridge. A novel. 224 pp.
ISBN 0-930044-26-6 $6.95

This Is Not for You by Jane Rule. A novel. 284 pp.
ISBN 0-930044-25-8 $7.95

Faultline by Sheila Ortiz Taylor. A novel. 140 pp.
ISBN 0-930044-24-X $6.95

The Lesbian in Literature by Barbara Grier. 3d ed. Foreword by
Maida Tilchen. A comprehensive bibliography. 240 pp.
ISBN 0-930044-23-1 $7.95

Anna's Country by Elizabeth Lang. A novel. 208 pp.
ISBN 0-930044-19-3 $6.95

Prism by Valerie Taylor. A novel. 158 pp.
ISBN 0-930044-18-5 $6.95

Black Lesbians: An Annotated Bibliography compiled by
J. R. Roberts. Foreword by Barbara Smith. 112 pp.
ISBN 0-930044-21-5 $5.95

The Marquise and the Novice by Victoria Ramstetter. A novel.
108 pp. ISBN 0-930044-16-9 $4.95

Labiaflowers by Tee A. Corinne. 40 pp.
ISBN 0-930044-20-7 $3.95

Outlander by Jane Rule. Short stories, essays. 207 pp.
ISBN 0-930044-17-7 $6.95

Sapphistry: The Book of Lesbian Sexuality by Pat Califia. 2nd
edition, revised. 195 pp. ISBN 0-930044-47-9 $7.95

All True Lovers by Sarah Aldridge. A novel. 292 pp.
ISBN 0-930044-10-X $6.95

A Woman Appeared to Me by Renee Vivien. Translated by
Jeannette H. Foster. A novel. xxxi, 65 pp.
ISBN 0-930044-06-1 $5.00

Cytherea's Breath by Sarah Aldridge. A novel. 240 pp.
ISBN 0-930044-02-9 $6.95

Tottie by Sarah Aldridge. A novel. 181 pp.
ISBN 0-930044-01-0 $6.95

The Latecomer by Sarah Aldridge. A novel. 107 pp.
ISBN 0-930044-00-2 $5.00

VOLUTE BOOKS

Journey to Fulfillment	by Valerie Taylor	$3.95
A World without Men	by Valerie Taylor	$3.95
Return to Lesbos	by Valerie Taylor	$3.95
Desert of the Heart	by Jane Rule	$3.95
Odd Girl Out	by Ann Bannon	$3.95
I Am a Woman	by Ann Bannon	$3.95
Women in the Shadows	by Ann Bannon	$3.95
Journey to a Woman	by Ann Bannon	$3.95
Beebo Brinker	by Ann Bannon	$3.95

These are just a few of the many Naiad Press titles. Please request a
complete catalog! We encourage and welcome direct mail orders from
individuals who have limited access to bookstores carrying our publications.